REMOTE CONTROL

NNEDI
OKORAFOR
REMOTE
CONTROL

A TOM DOHERTY
ASSOCIATES BOOK
NEW YORK

REMOTE CONTROL

Copyright © 2020 by Nnedi Okorafor

Edited by Lee Harris

A Tordotcom Book
Published by Tom Doherty Associates
120 Broadway
New York, NY 10271

www.tor.com

Tor® is a registered trademark of Macmillan Publishing Group, LLC.

The Library of Congress Cataloging-in-Publication Data is available upon request.

ISBN 978-1-250-77280-0 (hardcover)
ISBN 978-1-250-77279-4 (ebook)

Our books may be purchased in bulk for promotional, educational, or business use. Please contact your local bookseller or the Macmillan Corporate and Premium Sales Department at 1-800-221-7945, extension 5442, or by email at MacmillanSpecialMarkets@macmillan.com.

First Edition: January 2021

Printed in the United States of America

0 9 8 7 6 5 4 3 2

REMOTE CONTROL

CHAPTER 1

SANKOFA

"You come at the king, you best not miss."
—Omar Little, *The Wire*

The moon was just rising when Sankofa came up the dirt road. Her leather sandals slapped her heels softly as she walked. Small swift steps made with small swift feet. When she passed by, the crickets did not stop singing, the owls did not stop hooting and the aardvark in the bushes beside the road did not stop foraging for termites. Yards behind her, in the darkness, trotted the small red-furred fox rumored to follow her wherever she went. This type of creature wasn't known to live in Ghana, but stranger things were always afoot when Sankofa was around.

Sankofa was fourteen years old, but her petite frame and chubby cheeks made her look closer to ten. Her outfit was a miniature version of what the older more affluent Mamprusi women of northern

Ghana wore—a hand-dyed long yellow BioSilk skirt, a matching top embroidered with expensive lace, and a purple and yellow headband made of twisted cloth. She wore the gold hoop earrings, too. She'd done the head wrap exactly as her mother used to when her mother visited friends. Beneath the head wrap, Sankofa covered her bald head with a short-haired black wig. She'd slathered her scalp with two extra coats of the thick shea butter she'd recently bought, so the wig wasn't itchy at all. She also applied a thin layer to her face, taking care to massage it into where her eyebrows used to be. Despite the night's cloying heat, the shea butter and her elaborate heavy outfit, she felt quite cool . . . at the moment.

A young man leaned against a mud hut smoking a cigarette in the dark. As he blew out smoke, he spotted her. Choking on the last puff, he cupped his hand over his mouth. "Sankofa is coming," he hollered in Ewe, grabbing the doorknob and shoving the door open. "Sankofa is coming!"

People peeked out windows, doorways, from around corners and over their shoulders. Nostrils flared, eyes were wide, mouths opened and healthy hearts pounded like crazy.

"Sankofa come, ooooo!" someone shouted in pidgin English.

"Shia! Sankofa a ba!"

"Sankofa strolling!"

"Sankofa, *Sankofa, ooo*!"

"Here she comes! Aaa ba ei!"

"Beware of remote control, o! The most powerful of all witchcraft!"

"Sankofa bird landing!"

Women scooped up toddlers playing in the dirt and ushered their older children inside. Doors shut. Steps quickened. Car doors slammed and those cars sped off.

The girl called Sankofa walked up the quiet deserted road of the town that was pretending to be full of ghosts. Her face was dark and sweet and her jaw was set. The only item she carried was the amulet bag a juju man had given her five years ago, not long after she left home. It softly bounced against her hip. Its contents were simple: a roll of money that she rarely needed, a wind-up watch, a jar of shea butter bigger than a grown man's fist, a hand-drawn map of Accra, and a tightly rolled-up book. For the last week, her book had been an old old copy of *No Orchids for Miss Blandish*, a paper novel she barely understood yet enjoyed reading. Before that, a crumbling copy of *Gulliver's Travels*.

The town was clearly not poor. There were a few

huts, but they were well built and well kept. This night, though dark as a cave, Sankofa could see hints of bright light coming from within. These mud huts had electricity. People feared her but they still wanted to watch television. Beside them were modern homes, which equally feigned vacancy. Sankofa felt the town staring at her as she walked. It was hoping, wishing, praying that she would pass through, a wraith in the darkness.

She set her eye on the largest most modern-looking home in the neighborhood. The huge hulking white mansion with a red roof surrounded by a large white concrete gate topped with broken green bottle glass was easy to see. As she approached the white gate, she noticed a large black spider walking up the side. Its long strong legs and hairy robust body looked like the hand of a wraith.

"Good evening," Sankofa said in Mampruli as she stepped up to the gate's door. The spider paused, seeming to acknowledge and greet her back. Then it continued on its way up, into the forest of broken glass on top of the gate. Sankofa smiled. Spiders always had better things to do. She wondered what story it would weave about her and how far the story would carry. She lifted her chin, raised a small fist and knocked on the gate's door. "Excuse me, I would like to come in," she called in Twi. She wasn't sure how far she'd come. Better to stick to the language most understood. Then she thought better of it and switched to English. "Gateman, I have come to call on the family that lives here."

When there was no response, she turned the knob. As expected, it was unlocked. The gateman stood on the other side of the large driveway, near the garage. He wore navy blue pants, a crisp white shirt and a blank look on his face. He carried prayer beads, counting them along with shaking fingers. There was a light on over the garage and she could see his face clearly. Then he turned and spat to the side, making no move to escort her to the house.

"Thank you, sir," Sankofa said, walking to the large front door. The doorway light was off. "I will show myself in."

Up close, the house looked less elegant, the white walls were stained at the bottom with red soil, splashed there as mud during rainy season. There were large dirty spiderwebs in the upper corners where the roof met the walls. A shiny silver Mercedes, a white Tesla, a black BMW and a blue Honda sat in the driveway, the Mercedes plugged into the home's charger. The garage was closed. The house was dark. However, Sankofa knew people were home.

Something flew onto her shoulder as she stepped up to the front door. She stifled the instinct to crush it dead and instead, grabbed it and then opened her hand. It was a large green grasshopper. She'd seen this creature in one of the books she'd read. These were called katydids. She giggled, watching it creep up her hand with its long delicate green legs.

She softly glowed a vibrant leaf green. Not enough to kill, but enough to bathe the grasshopper in a shade of its own lovely greenness. If a grasshopper could smile this one did. She was sure of it. Then it hop-flew off. "Safe journey," she whispered.

She knocked on the door. "It is me," she called. "Death has come to visit."

After a moment, the front door lights came on. She looked up at the round ball of glass lit by the light bulb. Within minutes, insects would people the light. But not yet. A haggard-looking tall man in a black suit and tie slowly opened the door. The lights turned on behind him and she could see ten well-dressed adults, some in traditional clothing, others in stiff Western attire, all pressed together, wide-eyed and afraid. Cooled air wafted from the opened door and it smelled like wine, champagne, goat meat and jollof rice. The air-conditioner and the house cooks were working hard tonight. The hallway was decorated with shiny red and green trimming and fake poinsettia flowers, a plastic ornamented Christmas tree at the far end.

"I hope I am not interrupting your Christmas party," Sankofa said in English. She blinked. *Was* it Christmas? Or maybe still Christmas Eve? She felt a muffled yearning deep in her chest. She pushed the feeling away as she always did, thinking, *We never celebrated Christmas, anyway.* Though some in her hometown had. She remembered.

"No, no," the man jabbered, smiling sheepishly. "Chalé, p-please. Come in, my dear. Happy Christmas, o." He wore a silver chain with a crucifix around his neck. The crucifix rested on his shoulder. He'd just put it on, probably as he rushed to the door. Sankofa chuckled.

"Happy Christmas, to you all, too," she said. "I won't stay long. I am going to get something of mine that I've been searching for for years."

The solid marble floors were cool beneath her bare feet. The walls were covered with European-style oil paintings of European rustic landscapes. Sankofa wondered what trouble these people went through to get these paintings all the way out to this small suburb of Accra. And she wondered if it was worth it; the paintings were quite ugly. A large family photo hung on the wall, too. It was of a tall fat man, a fat woman with one fat son and two fat daughters. Happy healthy content people and definitely "been-tos." If she had to guess, she'd say from America.

In the dining room, Sankofa was asked to sit at a large table laden with more food than she'd glimpsed in weeks. It was nearly obscene. And what a surprise. She'd never imagined that been-tos ate so many native dishes. Kelewele, aponkye nkrakra and fufu, kenkey, waakye, red red, jollof rice, fried chicken, akrantie and goat meat, too much food to get her eyes around. "Oh chalé," she muttered to herself. Behind her, the house party came in and stood around her.

A young woman set an empty plate before her. She wore a uniform similar to the gateman's—a white blouse and navy-blue pants. "Do you . . ." The woman trailed off, her eyes watering with tears. She paused, looking into Sankofa's eyes. Sankofa gazed right back.

"I would also like a change of clothes," Sankofa said. "I have been wearing these garments for a week."

The woman smiled gratefully and nodded. Sankofa guessed the woman was about ten years her senior, maybe even fifteen. "Something like what you are wearing now?" the woman asked.

Sankofa grinned at this. "Yes, if possible," she said. "I like to wear our people's style."

The woman seemed to relax. "I know. We all know."

"My name is known here?" Sankofa asked, the answer being obvious.

"Very well," the woman said. The woman looked at the silent party. "Can someone call the seamstress?"

"It's already done," a fat woman said, stepping forward as she closed a mobile phone. Sankofa recognized her quickly. She looked a little fatter than she had in the family photo in the hallway. Life was good for her. "Miss Sankofa," the lady of the house said. "You'll have whatever garments you like within the hour." She paused. "The community has always anticipated a visit from you."

Sankofa smiled again. "That's good."

"You want orange Fanta, right?" the young woman in the uniform asked her. "Room temperature, not chilled."

Sankofa nodded. These were good people.

The Christmas party watched Sankofa eat. They were unable to sit down. Unable to even look at each other. Paralyzed. Sankofa was ravenous. She'd been walking all day.

She gnawed on a goat bone's remaining bits of meat and then dropped the bone on her plate. Then with greasy hands, she took her bottle of room temperature Fanta and guzzled the last of it. She belched as another was placed before her. The young woman popped the cap and stepped back.

"Thank you," Sankofa said, taking a gulp. She picked up another piece of spicy goat meat, paused, then turned to the silent party. "Are there any children in the house?" she asked. "I would like some company."

She nibbled on her piece of goat meat as the adults fearfully whispered amongst themselves. It was the same wherever she visited. They always whispered. Sometimes they cried. Sometimes they shouted. Always amongst each other. Away from her. Then they finally went and got the children. They knew they had no choice. This time was no different.

A plump boy of about ten and an older taller girl about Sankofa's age, shuffled in. The girl's mother, the lady of the house, had to shove the girl in. They wore their nightclothes and looked like they'd been dragged out of bed. They plopped themselves across from her at the table. The boy eyed the plate of fried plantain.

"So what are your names?" Sankofa asked. When they both just stared at her, she spoke in English. "So what are your names?" she asked again.

"Edgar," the boy said. Sankofa blinked. He spoke like an American, so she'd been right in her assessment. Americans were always so well fed.

The girl muttered something Sankofa couldn't catch. "What?" Sankofa asked.

"Ye," the girl whispered. She spoke like an American, too.

"It's nice to meet you," Sankofa said. "Do you know who I am?"

"You're Sankofa, the one who sleeps at death's door," Edgar said. He eyed her as he slowly took a slice of fried plantain. Sankofa took another few of the oily slices, too. They were sweet and tangy. Edgar seemed to relax when he saw that she enjoyed the same food as he did. Ye didn't move.

"You should get a plate," Sankofa said. Before Edgar could look around, the young woman placed a plate before each of them. The girl took all of two plantain slices and the boy loaded his plate with plantain and roasted goat meat. Sankofa liked the boy.

"You don't look as ugly as they say you look," he said.

Sankofa laughed. "Really?"

"No," he said, biting into some goat meat. "Your outfit reminds me of my mom."

"Reminds me of mine, too," Sankofa said. "That's why I wear it."

They ate for a moment.

"So what'd you get for Christmas?" she asked.

"We haven't opened presents yet," he said, laughing. "It's Christmas Eve."

"Oh." She fixed her eye on the girl. "Ye," she said.

The girl jumped at the sound of her name.

"I'm not going to kill you," Sankofa said.

"How do I know that?"

Sankofa rolled her eyes, annoyed. "You're not very good company."

After a pause, Edgar asked, "Don't mind my sister. She never likes coming to Ghana. She'd rather just be a boring American and stay in boring America." When Ye hissed at him, he hissed back. Sankofa laughed with glee.

"Where is your famous fox, the Movenpick?" Edgar asked. "Is it outside?"

"Probably," she said. "Yes."

"Was he someone's pet? In your village?"

"No. Just an animal who wanted to be free." Sankofa frowned and looked away.

"S-sorry," Edgar quickly said. "I didn't mean to bring up your . . ."

"It's fine. That was a long time ago now."

Edgar nodded and then leaned forward. "We only hear about you from our cousins," he said. His eyes narrowed and he lowered his voice. "So is it true? Can you . . ."

"Can I what?" Sankofa asked, cocking her head.

He glanced at his sister. She'd stopped eating and was frowning deeply at him.

"I can," Sankofa said. "You want to see?"

The party adults moaned. "This boy is a real idiot," she heard one of them grumble. "You don't tempt the devil!"

"Chalé, make him shut up!" someone else whispered. "He's going to get us all killed."

Sankofa glanced at the adults and then looked piercingly at the kids before her. She smirked. "Turn off the lights then." The boy jumped up, ran and shut the lights off. She smiled when she heard him snatch his arm from his protesting mother and retake his seat across from her. In the past, it had been difficult to control and there had been terrible consequences. However, this was not the case any longer. These days, it was like flexing a muscle.

Right there in the darkness, she glowed her dim green. Ye, tears freely rolling down her cheeks. The boy's eyes were wide and he had an enormous grin on his face. "Real life 'remote control'!" he whispered. "Wowolo!"

"Shush," a woman hissed from the group of adults. "No ghetto talk."

"Oh come on, Mom," Edgar said, rolling his eyes. "First I can't say 'chalé,' now this? Why even bring us to Ghana?"

Sankofa relaxed herself and her glow faded and then winked out. Someone immediately flipped the lights on.

"What is this town called?" she asked, getting up.

"Tah . . . tamale . . . sorry, I can barely pronounce it. There's an American food with the same name. T-a-m-a-l-e," Edgar said.

"Relax, Ye," Sankofa said. "You won't see me here again."

Ye wiped the tears from her face. "I hate this country," she said. Then she got up and ran out of the room. Sankofa and Edgar looked at each other.

"So where are you going next?" Edgar asked.

"To a place I'm not even sure exists anymore," she said. Sankofa smiled, glad that he had not run like his sister. She hated when that happened. It always made her feel that ache she worked so hard to mute.

"Why?"

She shrugged. "It's time."

"So, you really can't ride in cars?"

She shook her head.

"That's so cool," he whispered.

"Not really."

"Are you a child of the dev . . ."

"No," she snapped. The conversation ended there.

Sankofa left the house an hour later having eaten her fill, taken some leftovers, and showered. She'd traded *No Orchids for Miss Blandish* for another paper novel Edgar insisted she read, titled *Mouse Guard*. He said he'd gotten it from the trip his family recently took to the UK and though it was one of the only paper books he owned, she could have it. She hadn't wanted to take such a precious item from him, but he insisted.

She walked up the empty dirt road, now wearing a brand-new blue and white wrapper, matching top and headband, all made of soft, weather-treated BioSilk. She held her head up and looked into the night with the confidence of a leopard. Sankofa liked to imagine that she was a Mamprusi princess walking the moonlit road toward her long-lost queendom. If she had to guess, her mother would have been proud of the way she chose to carry herself . . . despite it all.

"I'm almost there, Mama," she muttered, clenching her fists. A twinge of anxiety about the incident in the road days ago. Then the feeling was gone. Onward. It had been way too long.

She stopped, hearing footsteps behind her. She

whirled around. It was the gateman from the house she'd just left. The one who had looked at her as if she were a smear of feces on some child's underwear.

"Anyén!" he cried. He switched to English. "Evil witch!" He was sweating and weeping. "Kwaku Agya. Do you know this name? Do you remember my brother's name? Does the child of the devil remember the names of those it kills?"

"I know the name," she said. Sankofa remembered all the names of those she took as a kindness.

Surprise and then rage rippled across his face. He raised something black in his hand. *Bang!*

Time always slowed for her during these kinds of moments. The misty white smoke plumed from the gun's muzzle. Then the bullet, this one golden, short and dented. It flew out of the gun's muzzle followed by a larger plume of white smoke. The bullet rotated counter-clockwise as it traveled toward her. She watched this as the heat bloomed from her like a round mushroom. In times like this, it was near involuntary. From somewhere deep within her soul, a primal part of her gave permission to her unearthly power. That part of her had been on the earth, walking the soils of the lands now known as Ghana for millennia.

The night lit up.

The empty road.

The trees.

The houses and huts nearby.

The eyes of the silent witnesses.

The gnats, mosquitoes, flies, grasshoppers, beetles, some in flight, some not. The hiding, always observing spiders. The birds in the trees. The lizards on the walls. And the grasscutter crossing the road a few feet away. Movenpick the fox standing nearby, never far from Sankofa's heels. Washed in light that did not come from the moon.

The corona of soft green light domed out from Sankofa. To her, it felt like the shiver of a fever. It left a coppery smell in her nose. The bullet exploded feet from her with a gentle *pop*! The molten pieces flew into the flesh of a palm tree beside the road.

Sankofa shined like a moon who knew it was a sun. The light came from her, from her skin. It poured from her, strong and controlled. It washed over everything, but it was only hungry for the man who'd shot at her. It hadn't always been this way. In the past, her light's appetite had been all-consuming.

The man stumbled back. The gun in his hand dropped to the ground. Then he dropped, too.

Sankofa walked up to him, still glowing strongly. She knelt down, looking into the gateman's dying eyes. She spoke to the man in his native language of Twi, "Your brother's name was Kwaku Samuel Agya and his cancer was so advanced that it had eaten away most of his internal organs. I did not cause this cancer, gateman. I happened to walk into his village when he was ready to die. He asked me to take him. His wife asked me to take him. His son asked me to take him. His best friend asked me to take him." Tears fell from her eyes as she spoke. Then she pushed away the pain in her chest. She muted it as she'd learned to do over the years. Her tears dried into trails of salt as her skin heated. She stood up. "When was the last time you spoke to your brother, gateman?"

His skin crackled and peeled as it burned orange. It blackened, flaking off into dust. His entrails spilled out in a hot steaming mass when his skin and abdominal flesh burned away. Then that burned, too. The muscle and fat from his limbs flared up and then fell to ash, as well. There was little smoke but the air began to smell like burning meat. A mysterious wind came and swept away the ash and soon all that was left was one bone.

"I will never know or understand what that is," she whispered. "But at least it's clean."

The bone dried, its surface snapped in several places, splintered and then cooled. Someone would find it.

"Now you will talk to your brother," Sankofa said. She turned away, opened her bag and brought out the jar of thick yellow shea butter. She scooped out a dollop. She rubbed it in her hands until it softened then melted. Then she rubbed it on her arms, legs, neck, face and belly. She sighed as her dry skin absorbed the natural moisturizer. She glanced at Movenpick who stood in the bushes to her right. The fox walked up the road, leading the way. Sankofa followed the fox into the night as if she were her own moon.

STARWRITER

F or the first five years of her life, Fatima was a sickly child. Mosquitoes adored her blood and so she had malaria every few months. But she still found ways to be happy. When she was well and old enough to crawl into the open area in back of the house, Fatima discovered dirt. She would sit beneath the large shea tree that grew closest to her family's small house and revel in the earthy smell of the dirt. She'd sift it between her fingers when it was dry and mold and squeeze it when it was moist. She especially loved to draw in it and the bigger her drawing, the more delighted she was with the dirt.

One evening, Fatima was outside with her grandfather. She'd been carving one of her giant circles in the mud around the shea tree. She sat back, satisfied, and looked up at the darkening sky. And that was when she discovered the stars. They were twinkling and blinking and shining like insects and tiny fish all in the same space. Her grandfather had always been a star gazer and her intense interest in the stars delighted him. He'd taught her all she knew, coming over more often to spend time with her in the evening and show the little girl that space was amazing. Before long, she'd learned the location and names of the constellations, though she sometimes preferred to name the stars herself. Jupiter, Mars, Venus and Milky Way were nice names, but "white spark," "palm kernel," "owusu" and "spiderweb" were better.

Her grandfather started calling her Starwriter because she claimed that though she couldn't read them, she could see and even write words she saw in the sky. But the name never stuck and Fatima remained Fatima and the name Starwriter was quickly forgotten. Still, she wrote what she saw in the sky on those evenings with her grandfather and those led to the most intricate designs a four-year-old could ever draw. They were the size of the entire yard, wider than the shea tree's circumference. Loops, spirals, branching designs, giant circles and sharp deep lines. Fatima was enjoying herself.

It was strange but it kept her occupied, quiet and exercised, so her parents didn't mind. At some point, she started climbing that shea tree to get a better look at her "sky words." She'd stay up there, marveling at what she'd made. Even when she wasn't feeling so well, she could usually be found amongst the tree's branches, gazing down at her work.

Then came that day, the day she unknowingly stepped onto the path to becoming the infamous Sankofa. She'd drawn one of her "sky words" in the large area of dirt beside the tree and then climbed up to look down at it. The constellation that her grandfather called Sagittarius had guided her hand. But tonight, a playfulness had made her see it differently. Like new. Writing it upside down, it made more sense. And then she'd added the flourish from the part of the constellation that had never been there until tonight. She giggled, delighted by her work. The sky words looked like a Sankofa bird! She looked back into the sky to make sure she'd gotten the design right. And that's when she saw what her brother Fenuku later called a "meaty shower."

A minute later, Fenuku dashed out the back door and Fatima saw him gather with his friends nearby to watch it. She'd climbed higher in her tree for a better look. Even her parents came outside to watch. The whole village would talk about it for weeks because not only were there beautiful green streaks decorating the sky, but one could actually hear the "shower" hitting the shea tree leaves like rain. One had even zipped down and hit the dirt at the base of the tree, right at the end of the swirl of one of her sky words.

Fatima climbed down to see if she could find it. There it was, like a tiny Sankofa bird egg or . . . seed. It glowed a bright green like a star. She paused for a moment, wondering about the "sky words," then she giggled, rushed forth and grabbed it. It wasn't hot to the touch, but as she'd held it to her eyes, she could see that its light was seeping from it like oil. She cupped it in her hands and the light pooled in her palm and seemed to absorb into her skin. It burned and she hissed. Maybe it *was* hot. She dropped the thing and it sank right into the soil, like a stone into water. She got to her knees, saying, "No no no, come back! I'm sorry! Come back, little seed!" But it was gone.

Fatima never told her parents or her brother because she was sure none of them would believe her. About a year later, maybe even exactly a year, that afternoon, when she was five years old, bothered with malaria-caused fever and aching muscles, she'd still managed to climb into the tree and sit on one of the top branches. It had been a while since she'd drawn "sky words." Her grandfather had passed away months ago and she no longer looked at the sky so much, and so she no longer drew what she saw. Now she spent her time playing with her dolls in the tree or just hanging from its branches.

She rested her head against the tree's trunk and shut her eyes. She loved this tree so much and every so often, it seemed to love her back, too, its leaves looking greener in the sunshine than any other tree. A cool breeze blew and being up here, she felt it directly. She was supposed to be in bed, but her mother was talking to her best friend, Auntie Karimu, on the other side of the house and Fatima had taken her chance.

She'd giggled because on the other side of the tree, she saw the red-furred animal curiously looking at her as it rested on a thick branch. The fox who'd escaped from the zoo two weeks ago and had in the last few days decided to make this tree its home. He was another reason she spent time in the tree. She'd been sitting between her mother's knees having her hair braided when the brief news story played on her mother's tablet. She and her mother had giggled about it because the news story had described foxes as crafty. "They'll never find that thing," her mother had said.

The breeze blew harder, rustling the fox's fluffy coat and feeling wonderful on her hot sweaty skin. Something below caught her eye. When she saw the soil churning, Fatima wondered if she was having one of the visions she often had when her malaria fever got high. Her furry friend on the branch across from her whined and moved further up the tree. Fatima, however, climbed down to investigate.

Maybe it's a mole, she thought. *Or a spider.* She hoped it was a spider; she liked spiders. Whatever it was, if it was coming up at the base of the tree, it had to be something good, for this was where the seed from the sky had fallen. Because of the seed from the sky nothing bad or scary could ever come close to this tree, at least that was how Fatima understood it. Even her father knew this tree was a good good tree; sometimes he even laid his prayer mat right on the spot where the thing was ascending.

What she immediately noticed as her bare feet touched the ground was the smell. Her parents had been traders until they acquired a small shea farm years before she was born. Today, their small farm extended a quarter of a mile from the house and Fatima was quite familiar with the tree's fresh scent, but this one always had a stronger nuttier aroma than the others. And now it smelled as if a whole truckload of sliced shea fruit had been dumped at her feet. Even in the strong breeze, it was powerful and heavy.

She wiped sweat from her brow as she stared down. The red soil was churning as if small hands beneath it were stirring and kneading the earth. The soil sank down and a hole about the size of both of Sankofa's five-year-old hands appeared. Then something flat and brown was pushing through it. She stood there fascinated. A wooden box. About six inches long and four inches wide and two inches deep. There was no latch, no lock, and it was a rich brown like the tree's trunk, though the wood was smooth, not the spongy rough of the shea tree.

"Oh!" Fatima whispered as she bent down to pick it up. "Is it for me?" Of course it was. She claimed it immediately, or maybe it claimed her. It was something valuable, or maybe it saw the value in her. It was beloved like something she'd lost a long time ago and just found, or maybe it had found her. It was like something she would own in a future life. Yes, oh yes, it was definitely hers.

She picked up her box. It was surprisingly heavy and she had to cradle it to her chest. She froze, staring at the hole. The box had been resting on a tannish-white root about as thick as three of her fingers put together. "Thank you," she said to it.

She sat down. Then she pushed up the box's thick lid. A hearty scent of crushed leaves rushed out and her eyes began to water at the sight of what was inside. Oblong in shape, it was just a little larger than her father's big toe and it had a smooth almost tooth-like surface. It was no longer leaking the glowing green light, but it was definitely the seed that had fallen from the sky and sunken into the dirt. "You've come back to me!" she said to the seed. And as if it had been waiting for these words, the root that had presented it glided back into the soil.

When she picked the seed up, her fingers went numb and she felt a warmth spread all over the rest of her body. She held it to her eyes as a green mist like incense smoke wafted from it. She laughed, blowing at and sniffing the mist; it too was warm. When she opened her mouth, she found she exhaled the green mist a bit, too. After a minute, the mist disappeared and the smell went away. Fatima giggled, cupping the seed in her hands, imagining it to be delicate and alive like a baby mouse.

"Hello," she whispered to it. "I'm Fatima. Maybe you like the heat from my hands. I have a fever from malaria, so I'm not feeling very well." She set the seed back in the box and shook out her hand until the feeling returned. Then she shut the box and got up. She used her sandal to push soil over the hole the root had left and took the box and its seed inside. By the time she stepped into her bedroom, her fever was gone. She simply didn't feel it anymore. The next day, even her parents were sure that her bout with malaria had passed.

As the days rolled on, her parents and brother came to know of the wooden box she liked to keep in her room. Her father would joke about the box with his friends, saying his imaginative daughter said the tree gave it to her. Her mother would talk about it at the market, saying her daughter treated everything like a person, even things she dug up from the ground. Her brother only rolled his eyes when he saw his sister playing with it. Fatima told the seed stories, she climbed into the tree with it, she snuck it to school in her pocket. "It doesn't have a face or a name," her mother had jokingly said one evening as she tucked Fatima into bed. "What is it with you and that old thing?"

"It's *my* thing," Fatima said importantly. "A nice thing that listens."

Nevertheless, though she didn't know it then, finding that seed in the box was the beginning of so much. She loved her favorite tree, shared its space with a fox who didn't belong in Ghana, and because her bouts with malaria had passed, she was a happier child. No matter how late she stayed in that tree, mosquitoes no longer bit her. She was well enough to make friends and go with them to watch her older brother Fenuku play football on the nearby field. Life was nice and fun and happy for Fatima that year.

Her parents didn't ask where she'd gotten the seed in the box. To them, it was just a thing. Maybe it was just a petrified palm tree seed she'd found somewhere in the shea tree farm and polished up. Maybe a teacher at her school or someone in the market dropped the box. Maybe it was an old jewelry box; her parents had lived in their small house since before both Fatima and her brother's births and there were certainly many forgotten random things in that house. It was all possible and normal. Her brother wasn't interested in the seed either. It was a thing that you didn't plug in, a thing that couldn't connect to the internet. To him it was a *boring* thing.

Almost a year to the day later, Fatima was in the tree brooding. She'd had an argument with her brother over a chocolate bar their father had told them to share. Her brother had snatched it and run off and just then, the politician had arrived and her parents were in no mood to hear her pleas for justice.

She climbed to the highest part of the tree, which was pretty high because she was so small and light.

And from here, she could see over the house and thus had a good view of the strangers who'd come to the house. She wiped away the frustrated tears in her eyes as she stared. There was a black SUV, parked in front of the house. She squinted. Two men were talking to her parents, a man wearing a white kaftan and pants and a heavy-set man dressed in a European suit. She immediately recognized the suit and gasped with delight. "How can this be!" she exclaimed.

She'd seen him on the jelli telli in the Village Square when the men gathered to discuss politics and current affairs. This was a politician known for shouting and wearing gold shoes. Her father found this man incredibly annoying. Fatima loved when he came on TV because the way her father talked about him made her and everyone in the room laugh. She squinted and sure enough, his shoes glinted so brightly, they looked made of sunshine. She giggled. Her brother would be so jealous when she told him what she saw.

Suddenly, the man in the white kaftan turned and seemed to look right at her. Fatima ducked down behind a branch, a shiver running up her spine. They all went inside and Fatima waited there for a few minutes wondering if she should climb down and hide amongst the shea trees in the farm behind the house.

"Hello," someone said from directly below.

Fatima hugged the branch she was already clutching even tighter. When she looked down, she saw that it was the man in the white kaftan. He was tall and even with his kaftan she could see that he was quite muscular, like one of those men who guards superstars. He had a black patch over his right eye and he was grinning up at her with the fakest grin she'd ever seen. His shoes reminded Fatima of walnuts.

"Good afternoon," Fatima said, still frowning.

"Your mother told me you like roasted goat meat and she gave me some to give you," he said, holding up a brown paper bag. "Why don't you come down so we can talk?"

"I'm fine up here, thank you."

"Don't be afraid, it's not a big deal. You found something buried here some time ago. Your mother and father told me."

Fatima suddenly wished she could jump out of the tree, dodge the man and run to her room. She'd slam the door and lock it. Then she'd grab the box with her seed and climb out the window. But she didn't think she could escape this man. So instead she said, "I don't know what you're talking about." In her mind she added, *And I didn't find it, it was given to me. It's mine.*

"Why don't you come down and we can properly

talk while you eat this?" he said, smiling grandly as he held up the bag again. "Your parents said I should ask you about the box, since it's yours."

When Fatima refused to move, his smile dropped from his face. "This is a waste of time. We'll find and take it. It's of better use to us than you. When my boss wins the election, even your little backward village will benefit from his policies. I was just being polite because I'm in such a fine mood." He turned and walked away. Fatima could barely contain the horror she felt, but she stayed where she was as he strode into the house through the backdoor.

Standing in the doorway, he suddenly whirled around and called up to her, "Do you believe in aliens?" he asked.

Fatima shook her head.

"Me, neither," he said. "But the LifeGen Corporation does and they can locate and track things using satellite and radar. Things like that odd meteor shower two years ago. They're inventing, but they're also always looking, watching, *hoping*. They pay good money. Money for campaigns." He brought a hand-sized device from his pocket and it immediately started pinging softly. "Ah, this will be easy." He turned and went inside the house as if he lived there.

Fatima waited for ten whole minutes. Then she

leaped down the branches, tumbled to the ground, jumped up and sprinted for her room. Inside, everything was exactly as she had left it. Except her box was gone. She ran to the front of the house and stopped in the doorway. Her parents and the politician with the gold shoes were laughing, talking, discussing. *But Daddy hates that politician,* she thought, utterly confused. She had never seen her father behaving like a completely different person before and it hurt her eyes. And *there* was her box, in the famous politician's hands.

Fatima shuddered as desperation and upbringing fought a violent battle within her mind. Upbringing won; a child was never to interrupt when adults were talking. And so in this way, six-year-old Fatima watched her father and the famous politician walk further up the road to discuss the sale of Fatima's box and the seed within it. She wasn't even called to say goodbye to it.

Later that night, her father said, "Fatima, don't sulk." He was beaming with glee. "That old box with your dried date in it, if you knew what Parliament Member Kusi paid for it. He's a terrible man, but his money is good."

"I think it was some kind of ancient artifact," her mother said, laughing as she set bowls of rice and stew on the table. "Fatima, be proud you dug it up. Maybe you'll be an archaeologist when you grow up and this will be the story you tell about how it all started."

"I didn't dig it up," Fatima insisted. "My tree *gave* it to me."

"You and that tree," her father said, laughing.

"It was mine! Now it's . . . it's out there in the world like a lost dog or . . ."

"That's enough, Fatima. I'll buy you that new dress you wanted. You've helped the family so much."

Fatima tried to hold her frown but she lost it at the thought of that wonderful blue dress Mrs. Doud had on display. It had flared sleeves and an embroidered collar. Fatima's frown melted into a pout and then to a smirk.

"See?" her mother said, poking her in the side. "It's good that we sold it."

"What about me?" her brother Fenuku asked.

"Were *you* the one who found it?" their father asked. Fatima grinned as her brother sulked.

"I'll buy you that tiny drone you wanted," their father said.

Fenuku's happiness was so brilliant that Fatima grinned even wider. As she bit into some roasted goat meat that her mother had prepared, though she still missed the seed, she felt better. It was for the best. Her father was right to sell the box. Fatima fell asleep quickly, her belly full as she clutched the plush brown rabbit her mother had bought her that evening. Still, she missed talking to the seed in the box. The plush rabbit didn't seem to hear a word she said.

Then came the strange news late that night. She only heard about it because she'd woken up and been unable to go back to sleep. After tossing and turning for two hours, she'd gotten up to play with her plush rabbit. "You are very nice," she told it as she sat on her bed. "But you're not like my seed." She paused, listening with her six-year-old ears.

"It's not my fault," the rabbit responded in a soft baby voice.

She smiled. "I know. But it doesn't change the fact. Adults never understand."

"Come on, let's play spaceship," the rabbit said.

And Fatima and the rabbit shot into space for a few minutes. The rebellion of playing with her new toy when she was supposed to be asleep gave her a bit of satisfaction. And for several minutes, she giggled amongst the stars. She froze, hearing footsteps outside her door. Then low voices. Frantic voices and then the sound of the front door opening and closing several times. Grasping her rabbit, Fatima jumped out of bed.

She peeked out and crept up the hallway to the

living room. No one. But she could hear voices outside. She ran across the room and peeked out the open window. Her parents and her father's best friend Kwesi were standing outside talking energetically.

"Are you sure?!" her father asked, clearly fighting to keep his voice down.

"I have a delivery man, Gustavus, who is stuck *right now* in traffic because the guy robbed Kusi right there in his car. They were stopped in the middle of the road!" Kwesi said. "A shiny black SUV. Gustavus showed me footage before the police arrived. You see the thief running away!"

"My goodness," her mother said. "Well, Parliament Member Kusi certainly has a lot of enemies."

Kwesi was shaking his head. "From my sources on the ground, it was his driver/bodyguard, that man you said was wearing the white kaftan. He took Kusi's credit cards, bank card, their phones, that thing you sold them, he even took Kusi's *gold shoes*."

Her father snickered. "I can just imagine him standing there all alone on the road in his socks. Serves him right for all the people his policies have harmed." He snickered harder. "I hope someone got photos."

Fatima leaned against the wall, stunned. Robberies existed, but as her father liked to tell her brother whenever he went outside to hang around with friends, "You're safe if you are not stupid. Know where to go and where not to go. And don't run around at night." But this man had just been at their house in broad daylight; her own father had willingly handed him her most prized possession. Now her box, the seed that had been gifted to *her* and no one else, was truly lost to the winds. Her father was still laughing when Fatima sadly slunk back to her room.

Fatima tried hard to forget the box with the mysterious seed inside. To put it all behind her. The politician never returned to demand his money back. That money bought a new truck to help haul shea fruit to the market, all her and her brother's school fees were paid off for the next four years. It was a dream come true, really.

Fatima was young and happy and if that had been that, she'd have forgotten the gift her favorite tree had given to her. Children heal quickly. However, that was not that.

CHAPTER 3

MOONRISE

Sankofa forgot her real name on the day that she lost everything. She was seven years old, a year older than she'd been when the box with her seed inside it had been sold and then lost. She'd been feeling hot all day.

High up near the top of the shea tree that grew beside her family's house, she'd been sitting in her favorite spot reading her favorite book, *World Mythology*. She'd read the book many times in the last year and today she was pretending to be the goddess Artemis and that her tree was a dryad. She tucked her book in the crux of a branch and climbed to the top of the shaggy tree. She gazed over the leaves. She could see the Zayaa Mosque from here. She could see her brother playing football in the field with some boys. She could see far and wide, possibly beyond her town of Wulugu. She'd never been outside of Wulugu, so she wasn't sure, but she liked believing what she saw was beyond it. The very idea of seeing beyond where she'd physically been made her feel powerful.

A wave of heat shivered across her skin and she felt a little weak. She looked down; it was a long way to the ground. Her mother was inside preparing dinner. Her father was across the dirt road visiting with friends. Neither of them liked her climbing the tree, even though the tree's fruits had been picked last week.

"I'm strong like Artemis," she whispered, looking down. This usually worked. But not today. She didn't even think it would work if she pretended to be the thunder gods of Shango, Amadioha or Zeus.

She dropped her book to the dirt and then climbed down, slowly, lightly resting her bare feet on the low oddly growing branch that made climbing the tree possible. She paused for a second as another wave of heat and light-headedness passed over her. As soon as it was gone, she moved faster. Best to get down before the weakness came back. A few feet from the ground, she jumped, landing silently.

She saw something red run off and shot a glance toward it just in time to see a flick of the animal's tail as it bolted around the house. She giggled. She'd seen the red-furred creature many times now, hanging around the tree. It caught and ate mice, lizards and other small creatures who lived amongst the shea trees, but it also liked to eat the shea fruit from her tree when they fell. Once or twice, she'd even seen it climb and sleep in the tree.

Fatima waited for the light-headedness to pass. She watched to see if the animal would peek around the corner as it often did after it ran away, but this time it didn't. When she felt better, she went looking for her mother inside. She smiled to herself; she'd been in the tree for an hour and no one would ever know.

"Mommy, I feel hot," she complained as she stepped into the kitchen, clutching her book. The smell of the soup made her stomach grumble. Her brother had caught a fat grasscutter and today they would feast on fufu and light soup with chunks of the rodent's meat.

Her mother pressed the back of her hand to her child's forehead. "I hope you are not coming down with malaria again, Fatima," her mother muttered. "Thought those days were over." It had been nearly two years since the last bout. She turned her hand over and pressed the back to Fatima's forehead. She flipped it and tried the back of her hand again. "You don't feel warm, praise Allah. Off you go."

Fatima put her book in her room and then went to find her brother. She wasn't surprised her skin didn't feel hot to her mother. It wasn't malaria at all. Malaria's fever felt like the heat came from within. Deep in her body. From her heart, lungs and tummy. This heat lurked on her skin, like warmed slick oil. It prickled and surged as if it would incinerate any malaria-carrying mosquito who had the nerve to try and bite her.

No, this was not malaria.

Nevertheless, what had been happening to her over the past year began to happen more intensely. Right now. Fatima stood at the edge of the field and cupped her hands. "Fenuku!" she hollered.

Her older brother turned at the sound of his name and the boy he was grappling with stole the football and took off with it. Fatima giggled as her brother stamped his foot hard on the dry grass and probably cursed. She was too far to hear exactly what he said. He still looked annoyed as he came jogging over. When he saw the look on her face, he froze.

"It's happening again," she said.

He put his hands on his hips. He was ten years old and tall for his age. Fatima's father always joked that when Fenuku was born he took all the height with him because Fatima was very short for her age.

"Oh yeah?" Fenuku asked, frowning at her as he caught his breath.

"Yeah," she said. "I feel real hot today."

"Ok, come on."

First Fenuku had her grasp a wasp. It always

started with a wasp. She hissed with pain as she felt it sink its stinger into her hand. She squeezed, feeling its rough body burst. The heat she felt flared with the pain of the sting. From the mosque's minaret, the muezzin began calling people to prayer. Her eyes shut, she focused on the muezzin's voice.

"Well?" she whispered after some moments.

"Yeah," her brother said, breathlessly.

"Oh goodness," she said. She didn't need to open her eyes, though. She could see it right through her eyelids. The green light. She could see the veins in her eyelids glow with it. Her skin felt as if every part of her was being gently grazed with needles. She breathed in and breathed out as she listened to the muezzin's soothing monotone prayers.

"Catch another," Fenuku suddenly said.

"Fenuku, it hurts so bad," she moaned. "Look at my hand." The swollen welt on her palm was an angry red.

"I know," he snapped. "But how else can we find out? Next, we'll try putting pepper in your eyes."

A part of her knew that her brother's requests were not right. She wasn't a science experiment. And she hated the pain. However, she was also curious. The same part of her that was curious to see what was outside of Wulugu was curious to see why whenever she felt this strange heat, pain caused her to . . . flare.

Fenuku said that he could *see* it happen to her. He said that she flashed a deep ugly green like a diseased moon and would pulsate a heat that reminded him of standing too close to a cooking fire. When she got like this, only slathering shea butter soothed her skin.

She looked at the hive, spotted a slow-moving wasp and caught it. It struggled in her hand, trying to escape. This wasp didn't want to harm her. She yelped as it finally stung her in the flesh between her right thumb and index finger. She moaned and opened her hand, letting it fly away. Her eyes watered.

"Oh!" her brother said. "That was a big one."

She met the dry eyes of her brother. After a moment, they both started laughing.

"Fenuku! Fatima!" their father called. He was on his way to the mosque. They ran over. Fatima made a fist with her swollen hand, not wanting her father to see it. She wiped sweat from her face.

"Come! Come!" He reached into his white robes and handed his mobile phone to Fenuku. "Buy me some cigarettes at the market," he said. "Pay attention to which you buy. You know the kind I like." Her father's only vice. It made Fatima want to both frown and smile. She loved her father, but she knew what her teachers taught her in school, too.

"Ok, Papa," her brother Fenuku said, taking the

phone and slipping it in his pocket. He looked at
Fatima and gave her a stern look.

"I wasn't going to say anything," she said. She wasn't.

"Just come on," he said, grabbing her arm.

As they walked to the market, Fatima thought
about the mosque. She was glad that she wouldn't have
to participate in salah for another few years. Not until
she hit something called The Puberty. It was hard for
her to sit still in the mosque. It was hard for her to sit
still anywhere except up in the shea tree.

But today, she wanted to be in the mosque. The
women and girls were always on one side, the men and
boys were on the other. She'd have had an excuse to
get away from her brother. Plus, she wanted to speak
to Allah in his house. She needed to pray.

*Ever the Most High, Mighty One, tell me what the light
is,* she thought as she followed her brother. *What does it
do? Is it because of the box the tree gave me? I didn't sell
it, Papa did.* She passed a hut inside which two women
were laughing really hard as they took a package from
a delivery drone. One of them wore jeans and a white
frilly blouse. She looked like a been-to. Fatima wondered if this was why the woman could laugh so hard
and freely, because she'd "been to" other places, seen
new things and the world was that much more enjoy-
able because of it.

Fatima envied her. She wanted to see what it was like outside of town, too. She often saw airplanes fly across the sky and she imagined just how far she could see if she stood on top of one of those as it flew faster than a dragonfly. Fatima would later understand that these things she thought as she walked were indeed prayers. Final prayers.

Her life was about to change.

The market was across the street from the only busy road that ran near Wulugu. Two lanes of pot-holed decades-old concrete. Fatima loved crossing it; it was like a game. The market gave her and her brother a reason to cross it fairly often, too. She grinned watching the cars, trucks and okada zoom this way and that, throwing up dust, garbage and exhaust. One day she'd be on one of those going who knew where, when she was older and had a job. But she didn't want a husband like the other girls. If she had a husband, she wouldn't be allowed to travel much. *I'll get my husband when I'm very old.* She giggled at her thoughts, despite the fact that she felt like she was melting and she could still feel the stinger in her hand.

"Come on," her brother shouted. He ran. But Fatima was looking at an approaching tanker. These vehicles always made her pause. She liked to imagine them as bombs on wheels. At her cousins' house, they had a jelli telli that could stretch across the room's entire wall. The whole village would come by to watch Hollywood movies about faraway places where terrible and wonderful things happened. And in many of those films, tanker trucks would blow up like giant heated palm kernels.

As her brother crossed the road, Fatima's gaze stayed on that tanker and she daydreamed about plumes of smoke, boiling orange, red and yellow flames, burning the very air it consumed. Before she knew it, her brother was halfway across. She gasped.

"Fenuku," she called.

He turned around. When he saw his sister still standing there, he threw his hands up with annoyance. Then he motioned for her to come. His actions were so dramatic looking that Fatima giggled.

"You can make it!" he called.

"Ok!" she called back, her heart pounding in her chest. A wave of heat rolled over her flesh and she wondered what those around her might have seen had they been looking at her. Nevertheless, few people noticed short dark-skinned little girls in dusty old purple and white printed dresses.

The tanker zoomed past, slapping her with gravel and a fresh plume of dust. She coughed as a woman beside her ran across. There was a gap in the traffic as a large group of cars approached. Fatima made a run for it. She laughed as she ran. Then she stepped into a pothole, stumbled and fell, skinning her knee. She felt herself pulse with heat from the pain and for this reason, she paused. The olive-green car was upon her before she even looked up. Her brother loved cars and Fatima had looked through the tattered car magazines his uncle brought him from Accra. In this way, she knew that the green vehicle barreling toward her was a BMW.

Fatima was flying.

She could see all the way to the city of Accra, though she'd never been there. Her mother said Wulugu was over three hundred miles away. But Fatima was that high in the sky now. She was finally seeing beyond her village. She wished she could tell her father about all she was seeing. Maybe when she landed.

Fatima heard the sound of blaring horns and smelled the smoke of screeching tires. She hit the ground, scraping the side of her face. People running to her. Her brother screaming her name, tears in his eyes. He'd never cried when the wasps stung her. "FATIMA!" he wailed, as he ran to her. "Sister!" He had never called her "sister." She chuckled and doing so hurt.

Her face was pressed to the concrete of the street. She felt the sunshine on her skin. Warming her skin. Warmth on warmth. The market was emptying as people poured out to see what had happened. Her brother was screaming. He was almost to her.

Then the pain came. This was the moment when Fatima forgot her name. It was a pain that tumbled to her soul. Later she would understand that it wasn't just a pain. It was a beginning. And this beginning annihilated all that came before it.

The red sharp aching radiated from her hip where the car had rammed her. She moaned deep in her throat. Something was coming. Then it burst forth. She was on fire and it was green.

She heard her brother sobbing.

A woman yelled, "What is . . ."

Fatima squeezed her eyes shut, feeling the blood strain in her ears. Then all went silent. Except the sound of idling vehicles.

When she opened her eyes, she gasped. Everyone was asleep. Her brother lay on the street. The woman who must have spoken, lay beside him. Everyone in the market, those who'd come out to see. A man in a car rolling to a soft stop. All asleep. Fatima's body flared again with pain. And this time she saw it. A corona of green sickly light burst from her, growing huge as it traveled from her small body. A bird dropped from the sky. A drone fell beside her and she vaguely wondered if it was the same one that had just delivered a package to those girls. A mobile phone on the ground burst into flames. No more cars or trucks came up or down the road.

Slowly, gently Fatima stood up. She touched her head. Her cap of short hair was gone. Her left eye twitched and her body began to shake so severely that she sat down hard on the concrete. Sweat poured down her now bald head and she could feel every drop. It gathered at her chin, dripping to the hot road. She stared at her brother who lay beside her. One of his shoes was half off and his white kaftan was smudged with dirt. His face was turned away from her.

It left her as a butterfly leaves a flower. She felt it go. It wasn't instant, just a gradual disappearance. Her name. She couldn't remember her name. She whimpered, fighting to recall it. Nothing. "Home, home, mommy, the tree," she whispered. "Fenuku's dirty room. Papa's cigarettes. Papa wanted his favorite cigarettes." Still nothing. No name.

She shut her eyes tightly and her mind fell on an image of Shango in her mythology book. He was standing in the clouds looking down at a big city in Nigeria, his hands on his hips as lightning crashed around him. She'd always liked this picture because he looked like a superhero, but was not. She didn't like this photo so much anymore. However, she opened her eyes. She rubbed them with steady hands. She slowly got to her feet.

She pressed at her hip. The pain was big, but it was not sharp. Her hip still worked. She was ok. She looked around. No one stirred. She limped home.

She passed the mosque. Inside, everyone was asleep. Including her father. They lay in various positions, some as if they were still praying, including her father, others simply lay this way and that. At home, her mother was asleep. This made her run down the hall and she somehow ended in her brother's room. On his table were the birds he liked to carve—an owl, a hawk and a Sankofa bird. She picked up the Sankofa bird and ran her finger over the long neck that looked backwards as it took an egg from behind it. She felt a prick of pain as a splinter from the wood entered her flesh and her body flashed with light. She dropped the bird and its neck snapped. Tears fell from her eyes to the floor as she knelt down and picked up the pieces. She'd broken the bird, just as she'd broken her family and her entire hometown.

She threw the bird down and left the room. In the kitchen, she made herself a plate of fufu and soup from the dinner her mother had prepared. She ate until she was fuller than she'd ever been in her life. Then she slept like everyone else in town. Come morning, everyone else was still . . . asleep.

CHAPTER 4

GODDESS OF TRAVEL

After three days at home, she had to walk. As she walked, she wept. Her mother, father and brother were dead and she now understood this deeply. The dust on her face made her eyes sting and itch.

She'd left her mother's body in the house. After a few days, it had started bloating. And then there was the smell. And the flies. They were all over Wulugu, sprouting from people's bodies like fidgeting black flowers. The house was suddenly full of them. Maggots wriggled everywhere. The newly hatched flies crawled on the walls, slow and bewildered, their wings fresh and moist. The adults beat themselves against the windows, copulated and laid more eggs in her mother and under the carpet. She hated the sight and sound of them. She would hate flies forever.

She found that when the flies really angered her, her body would glow, not heat, *glow,* and every fly in the room would drop dead. Her body did this many times when she crept into the main room to see her mother's corpse. But the flies always returned hours later. They emerged from her mother's body, from other rooms, from outside when she opened the door.

And so the seven-year-old girl in her pink knee-length skirt and yellow T-shirt gathered what food she could find, soap, her brother's Sankofa bird that she'd broken, her mythology book, her mother's favorite gold hoop earrings, a wooden owl her brother had carved for her, and a jar of her father's shea butter, put it all in the satchel she used for school and she walked up the road.

She stopped, turned back and went a last time into her parents' bedroom and took one of her mother's black curly-haired wigs to cover her bald scalp. It didn't fit her small head, but she wore it anyway, imagining it to be more like a hat she hid beneath.

"I am like Hermes," she said aloud as she stepped onto the quiet road, just to hear her voice. Hermes was a god of travel. Maybe she could find the box that her father sold away. The box that was taken from her and if it had not been taken, none of this would have happened. *It was mine*, she thought. And it was all she had left of home.

She nodded to herself as she walked, back straight, stride true. "I will find you. Wherever you are."

CHAPTER 5

THE ROAD

"Inshallah," she said to herself, over and over as she walked along the main road.

The same road where she'd been hit. The bodies, including her brother's, were still there. However, there was not a bit of traffic on the usually busy street. She ran alongside the road, not daring to look toward her brother's corpse. Not daring to look at any of the faces. The swarms of flies were so thick that she wouldn't have seen much if she'd looked, anyway.

Up the road, she passed three cars that had rolled into the bushes. Each was a nest of flies and rotting corpses. Other than these, there were no other vehicles. Eventually, after she'd walked for a half hour, she came to a roadblock in the distance. There were at least three soldiers in forest green fatigues standing at it. She hid in the grasses on the roadside and crept closer.

They stood in front of two thick slabs of yellow-striped concrete dragged into the road. Their military vehicles were parked on the side. And there was a white man with them who was wearing all black with a badge on the right side of his chest she couldn't quite see, like a secret police officer in one of the Hollywood movies. The white man's uniform was long-sleeved and it was hot and humid, but he seemed comfortable. She stepped into the shadow of the trees and grasses and snuck by. She was a small girl who'd spent all her life climbing the family shea tree. So she was fast, silent and comfortable amongst plant-life. Plus, they probably didn't expect to see any survivors, especially a little girl.

Once past the roadblock, she made a turn onto another road and she walked for two hours. And by the evening, the world opened up to her. She was outside Wulugu, in the town of Nabori. People. Homes. Markets. Cars and trucks. She spent that first night, however, in a cluster of trees beside the busy road. Exhausted, she fell into a deep sleep almost the moment she rested her head against the tree. The loud gasp of someone feet away woke her. "Ghost! Spirit!" a man whispered. He turned and stumbled off.

She froze, listening with every part of her body because it was too dark to see him clearly. He was moving away. Nearly gone. She breathed a sigh of relief, her whole body shaking with the rush of adrenaline.

She was many yards into the small forest beside the road. *How did he see me?* she wondered. Then she realized it. She was glowing, faintly green-yellow, but just enough to look like a forest spirit in the darkness. She couldn't see very well around her, but she was sure she was surrounded by dead mosquitoes and other biting insects. Maybe this was why she was glowing, because her body was being assaulted by their bites and it was protecting itself. She quickly rubbed fresh shea butter on her arms, legs and torso and grabbed her things.

Just after sunrise, as she walked alongside the road, a man driving a truck stopped beside her. She kept walking, pretending she did not see him. She was holding the wooden body of her broken Sankofa bird and she squeezed it, praying the man would just go away.

"Do you need a ride?" he asked.

Sankofa pressed her chin to her chest and kept walking.

"Hello?" the man said from his truck. "I am safe. I have three daughters about your age. It's not right for you to be walking here."

She kept walking, but he didn't go away. "I will call the police," he said, holding up his mobile phone.

"No!" she said, looking up. "No police, sir."

"Then where are you going?" he asked, grinning. He wore a long white kaftan and there were prayer beads hanging from his rearview mirror. "What's your name?"

She looked at her feet and shook her head. She muttered the first name to come to mind. "My name's . . . Sankofa. I'm going to the . . . next town." *Please don't ask me the name of it,* she frantically thought.

"Get in. I will drive you," he said. "I know a woman there who can offer you a bed to sleep in for however long you need. I'll even program my truck in front of you and have it drive itself, so you know exactly where I'm taking you."

She hesitated. The name "Sankofa" was echoing in her mind, filling empty confused crevices. She liked it. She put her brother's broken bird into her pocket and stepped toward his truck. She didn't trust the man, but she didn't want him to call the police, either. The thought of her dead parents, dead brother, dead town pulled at her. Maybe she *did* want him to call the police . . . so they could arrest and punish her for what *she'd* done. But she also wanted to flee, to escape, to keep going so she could right all the wrongs by finding the box. Yes, she thought, if she found the box maybe everyone would . . . wake up. "Ok," she said. "Just into town, though."

However, the moment Sankofa touched the truck's door, something happened. She felt nothing. She saw nothing. She heard nothing. The truck just stopped working. One moment its idling engine was chugging away, the next, it was not. There was no sigh, as it stopped. No exhalation of exhaust or steam. No electric spark. The truck simply was no longer running. There were no vehicles passing on the road at that moment, so the silence was profound.

"What did you do?" the man asked.

She stepped back as he climbed in and tried to start his truck. Nothing happened. Not even a vehicular gasp. The truck was simply dead.

"What'd you do?" he shouted again, as he turned the key and nothing happened. "Are you some kind of witch?" He tried again. Nothing.

"I didn't do anything," she said, stepping away.

The rest happened fast. She sensed the change in the man, from kind and helpful to furious. Swift like the weather. She turned and ran. She was fast, but this man was faster and she didn't get far before he'd grabbed her satchel. He yanked at it and she fell to the ground. "What did you do to my truck?" he shouted. "I was only trying to help you! My truck is my *livelihood*!" He slapped her hard across the face, his eyes wide and red.

The hot, raw sting registered in her brain and her body flooded with terror and panic. She stumbled backwards, holding her face. She remembered sneaking across the grass, as she stared at the roadblock. Leaving Wulugu. Seeing her mother's fly-riddled body. Her dead brother who'd just been alive beside her on the road. Then she was thrust forward and she glimpsed death, destruction, heat, violence and more terror. Then she was back staring into the bewildered eyes of a man who was about to slap her again.

The green light that burst from her was wilder and denser than what had happened in Wulugu, but it didn't travel beyond the man and his truck. She glanced at this for only a moment, then she pressed herself to the ground. The second blow from the man didn't come. There was no sound and only moments passed. She heard a vehicle zoom by on the road. When the vehicle didn't stop, she opened her eyes. She was in the shade of the dead truck, her satchel still on her shoulder. When she looked at where the man had been, all that was left was what might have been a jawbone. The top or bottom, she did not know. But it still carried all the teeth. She screeched and got to her feet. Sankofa ran.

She never made it to the nearest town, whatever it was called. Instead, before her feet took her there, she turned and walked into the bush. She stopped walking when it was nearly too dark to see. She cleared a spot in front of a tree and used some large old palm fronds to make a dry place. Then she curled up on them and fell right into a deep dreamless sleep.

When she woke the next morning, she remembered what happened and she started crying before she even opened her eyes. And when she finally did open them, they were gummy with dried tears and dirt. Eventually, she stopped crying and hunger pushed away her grief. After a search amongst the peaceful trees and bushes, she located a mango tree heavy with ripe fruit and a small secluded stream; her food and water concerns were solved.

As she bathed in the stream, she looked up and there was the fox who'd been skulking around her town. "You're alive, too!" she'd whispered happily. It stood on the other side of the stream staring at her, water dripping from its narrow muzzle. Then it trotted from the shallows into the bushes, disappearing into the shadows with a swish of its luxuriant red-orange tail. Even after it was gone, the forest felt that much friendlier and welcoming. Sankofa stayed in that forest for a week.

She spent most of her days rereading and rereading her mythology book and watching for the fox, whom she'd spotted another two times. Once, at dusk while she'd prepared her spot for sleep, she saw it peeking at her from behind a nearby tree. The second time was on her last night in the forest. At the time, she was sure she'd live in that forest forever, despite the fact that eating a diet of mangos, bananas and water grass gave her horrible diarrhea that kept her near the stream washing and washing after each bout.

She'd been so happy in that forest, away from everyone, not having to speak, being unseen, living in the moment and turning her back on the past. However, all of that day, the protective wall of denial she'd managed to put up had been gradually crumbling. She'd heard an especially loud truck pass on the nearby road and she started thinking about the man she'd killed. The man who'd slapped her and had been preparing to slap her again. He'd been a kind Muslim on his way to work and her presence had somehow changed him into a raging beast.

Soon she was constantly thinking of her family, her town, her home, all dead. She started to glow that night. And in the brightness of her heated body, she saw the fox looking at her, feet away. She was resting on the tree against which she liked to sleep. Her head on the tree's rough trunk, her mind unsettled.

"Hello," she said to it. The fox didn't move, though its pointy ears pricked and turned toward her. "You should have a name." She thought for a moment and smiled as the name bubbled up from her anxious memory. "Movenpick," she said. She'd seen a commercial for the Accra hotel on the news feeds and she'd always liked the sound of the word. "Movenpick," she said again. "That's your name." The fox licked its chops and looked around with its large gold-red eyes. "Do you want the box back, too? If I find it, will you then steal it from me?" she laughed, tired, a drop of sweat tumbling into her eye. "Will you eat it? Swallow it whole? I'll get the box back, if you come with me."

The fox turned and trotted off and Sankofa's smile dropped from her face. She crawled to her bedding, slathered fresh shea butter on her skin, and lay on it. It was another hour before she fell asleep and when she did, she dreamed about her mean old auntie Nana.

Her mean old auntie Nana had been educated in the West, made lots of money there and rarely visited Sankofa's father, her younger brother. However, when she did, she liked to sit in the main room with a steaming cup of coffee in the morning and talk at Sankofa and her brother about mean things in a mean way. In Sankofa's dream, it was one of those times, except her brother was not there, nor were her parents, and the main room was empty. Her old mean auntie Nana sipped from her large cup of boiling coffee and glared at Sankofa. "What kind of human being lives in the bush like an animal?" she asked in her nasally American English. "Stinking of shea butter over dirty skin."

Sankofa's voice was small. "Here I won't hurt anyone like I hurt Mommy and Daddy and Fenuku," she responded.

Then her old mean auntie Nana said what she'd said to Sankofa's father many times. "If I thought like that, I'd have never gone on to earn my PhD and become a physicist. I'd have been one of the sad bush women here, shackled to a husband and children." She slurped her coffee loudly. "If you hide forever, you'll never find anything. And there is one thing you know you want to find. Go and find it, stupid nonsense child."

When Sankofa awoke, her body was cool. And instead of fear of her mean old auntie Nana, she drew strength from the woman. She rubbed her eyes, got up and looked down at her dirty purple dress. Then she went to the stream and washed it as much as she could, laid it out to dry and then went back in to wash herself. She ran her hand over her bald head and told herself, *I will steal a wig that fits.* And some part of her was sure her old mean auntie Nana would approve and this made her feel stronger.

And so, while rubbing her bald head with shea

butter, she *tried*. She shut her eyes, took a deep breath
and reached out. The seed in the box had been long
gone for two years, sold and then stolen and then who
knew what, but it knew her and she knew it. She was
sure. She gasped. It was like a point of green light in a
dark familiar space. She couldn't see where it was, but
she knew. She could find it. *It's far, but it's not that far,*
she thought to herself. *A few towns away. Somewhere
cool, dry, dark. Inside something?*

Sankofa opened her eyes, tears rolling down her
cheeks. Then she had another thought, though she
wasn't quite sure what she meant by it. *I will stand up
straight.* And in that stream, all alone and naked, with
no family or loved ones, Sankofa stood up straighter.

Over the weeks, Sankofa learned that she couldn't
drive in vehicles or touch digital windows or mobile
phones, she couldn't even touch jelli tellis because
something about her killed technology. She was young
and alone, yet she was dangerous. It was mere nights
after leaving the forest that she had to kill another
man who first tried to take her satchel of things and
then tried to drag her into an alley. Some people may
have seen it happen because the next day, strangers
started giving her things. Some gave her money and

asked her to pray for their loved ones. Some of the market women gave her food (boiled eggs, sacks of plantain chips, groundnuts) if she promised to "keep death away." Most people simply avoided her. Word about Sankofa traveled fast, though it was never connected to Wulugu.

And she also learned that the seed kept moving, always one or two steps ahead of her. She arrived in the market where it had been kept in a refrigerated truck full of vegetables and meat for days before the truck left. "How did you know they parked and did their business right in this spot?" the old man who brought her here had asked.

"The seller's auntie told me," Sankofa lied, smiling to hold back her frustration. She'd have been here sooner if it weren't for the torrential rains that had turned the roads into shallow rivers of mud. Then she'd been a day late finding whoever had it again two towns away. Then a week later, learning that whoever had it took it towns away. And so on. She tracked it and followed, tracked it and followed. It was almost as if the seed had a will of its own and was playing with her. But she refused to believe it could be so malicious. One day, she would catch it.

In media outlets, word about the town of Wulugu did spread quickly, though. The government speculated

CHAPTER 6

THE RED COUCH
AND EYE PATCH

Sankofa lived this way for five years.

She pursued the seed around Northern rural Ghana, never telling anyone why she went where she went, moving about with earned and justified entitlement, listening for word of the seed in a box and allowing others to wrap her in the mythology of a spirit. People whispered things like, "She's the adopted child of the Angel of Death. Beware of her. Mind her. Death guards her like one of its own." There was truth in every single one of the stories.

Sankofa took shelter when she wanted shelter. She ate well because she demanded good food. And then, starting when she was about eleven years old, there were those who sought her out. There was the mother who came to Sankofa crying about her son who was in a vegetative state and had been on life support for eight years. There was the husband, daughter and mother of the woman suffering constant extreme pain from terminal stomach cancer. By this time, with effort, she could purposely call forth her light at very close proximity, enough to take a life. As long as everyone left the building. And in this way, Sankofa was able to give people what they needed and then moved on while they wept and pretended she wasn't there.

Her story travelled like an ancestor, always ahead of, beside and behind her. She made no friends, except for Movenpick the fox who continued to follow her at a distance. . . . and Selah the white tailless fastidious stray cat who travelled with her for three of those five years.

One terrible night, three men attacked Sankofa and Selah the cat as they slept in an empty market. They'd killed Selah, a man crushing the cat's head beneath a boot, kicked Movenpick when the normally evasive fox tried to intervene, and then Sankofa had killed them all. Afterwards, Sankofa stared at the bones of the dead men left behind, three jawbones and two long bones that could have been from arms or legs. Then she looked at Movenpick, who stood feet away, bruised but alive, despite the fact that Sankofa's light had washed over the creature like toxic water. She buried her beloved cat and continued on.

Sankofa survived. A seven-year-old on the road

alone, then an eight-year-old, then nine, ten, eleven. By the time she was twelve, most knew not to attack her and they gave her what she wanted and needed, instead. However, she spoke to no one about what drove her. What she was searching for. Who would understand? Who would care? She pursued the seed, which she eventually learned meant pursuing the man with the one eye across northwestern Ghana. The man who'd gone into her bedroom, taken the seed and then given it to the politician. The man who'd then stolen it from him, along with his money and golden shoes.

She was always ten steps behind the one-eyed man, as a girl on foot could only be when chasing someone moving around in a car or truck. She followed what it was that she saw behind her eyes when she closed them. The tiny green oblong moon that she could almost touch, so sure she was of its whereabouts. The problem was that it kept moving. The one-eyed man didn't rest anywhere long enough for her to catch up and so neither did the seed.

Sankofa followed it this way and that. Arriving in the exact spot where the seed had been in a car, in a suitcase, in a pocket, in a backpack, days or even weeks prior. Then she would be off again. On foot. For five years, she persisted with this slow pursuit. Striking fear, awe and stories into hearts, getting those items she believed she was owed, and mercifully taking lives from those who requested it along the way. Until the day in Tepa.

Malaria. Some part of Sankofa that she'd locked tightly away remembered it well. She knew it slowed a person down enough for anything one was running from to catch up. As she walked, she smacked her lips, but the dry taste still remained in her mouth. She frowned and flared her nostrils. For so many years.

She held her light in as she walked through the town. Today she wore a blue and white wrapper and top, the colors of water. She wore the big gold hoop earrings that had been her mother's and she now thought of as hers, despite the fact that she was still years too young to wear such earrings. She'd recently moisturized her skin with shea butter. Today would be a day of cleansing. She arrived at his home at sunset. It was a nice beige house with two Mercedes parked in front. Sankofa touched both of them as she made her way to the front door. She stepped up to the door and hadn't stood there for even ten seconds before it opened.

He had a red patch over his eye, he had a large gold watch weighing down his wrist, a thick gold chain around his neck, he wore a bloodred dress shirt and those stylish jeans that spoke more of wealth than actual fashion sense in Sankofa's opinion. "You, again. Come in," he said, stepping back and taking a sip of the brown liquid in the glass he carried. In his other hand he carried a burning cigarette.

Sankofa stared at him for a moment. After all these years, finally. She'd caught him. *But is he dying?* she wondered. The armpits of his dress shirt were damp with sweat. His face was shiny with more sweat. He leaned on the door as if he would collapse if he let go. His teeth were yellow. She stepped inside. "What is wrong with you?" she asked, following him down the hallway.

"As if you don't know," he said over his shoulder. "The Adopted Daughter of Death comes and asks what is trying to kill me. Oh the irony."

They entered a living room where there were a red couch and two red armchairs equally as red as the sweaty shirt he wore. He coughed and plopped onto the couch. The carpet probably used to be white, but it was now an uneven beige. "Welcome to my humble abode," he said. "One of my women lives here and takes care of it, but I come here when I am tired." He shut his eyes and moaned. "I'm so tired."

Sankofa glanced around the place and then sat in one of the armchairs and looked hard at him.

"No one is here," he said, his eyes still closed, rubbing

his hands down his face. "I sent my girl away two hours ago, told the houseboy not to come in today."

"Why?"

"Because I knew The Adopted Daughter of Death was coming to collect her debt. Why not just let me die of bad bad malaria, eh? Why come here with your nonsense trouble? Following and following slow slow, just leave a man to rest."

"You have something of mine," she said.

"So you make me sick to slow me down?"

"I don't make people sick."

"No, you just kill them."

"I only take life when people ask me to, when people are sick and in too much pain to live. The word is euthanasia . . . or when people threaten my life."

"Death's daughter, so merciful. Is that normal to you, though? Were you always like this? Poisoning people with some sort of body radiation that comes from your ovaries or whatever . . . it has to be a female thing, this type of witchcraft thing. Nothing else is believable." He seemed to be growing more and more delirious as he spoke. "It's evil, satanic, rain fire upon you in Jesus' name!"

"Why did you have to steal it?!" she shouted.

"Why not?" he said with a laugh. "Parliament Member Kusi was a fraud. He had me stealing it from you to give to LifeGen, that fucking big American corporation that's probably going to eventually destroy the world. Who knows what this seed thing is or does . . . the world should thank me."

Sankofa had heard of LifeGen in passing. In some of the hospitals where she'd taken lives. In the cancer wards. LifeGen made a lot of the drugs patients took. The LifeGen symbol was a hand grasping lightning. But clearly, their drugs didn't work very well. And clearly, pharmaceuticals weren't their only focus. "Where is it?" she asked.

"Not here!" he screamed. The action seemed to drain the rest of his energy. Sankofa groaned and let her head fall into her hands. She felt it now. She knew. Why hadn't she known *before*? It wasn't here. It was close but it wasn't here. "I've wanted to get rid of it since the day I stole it. What did I need with some artifact when I had bank cards full of millions in stolen money? You know I got half of that money out of those accounts before he was able to shut down the account within the hour. *That's* why I was on the run." He cocked his head and twisted onto his back. "But that damn seed thing . . . it had a *pull*. Couldn't sell it, throw it away, couldn't even leave it behind. Damned thing."

"Then why'd you just get rid of it?"

"I didn't! I lost it after I got sick and came here. It's been days." He suddenly sat up and pointed at her. "Now you show up *here*, instead of leaving me alone and following it. Evil evil goddamn thing."

Sankofa stood up. He pointed a gun at her. It must have been in the couch. He'd truly been waiting for her. "I was just leaving," she said.

"No. I'll never rest until I know you are dead," he said. "Five years of looking over my shoulder for a devil child. No more. I will get over this damn malaria, but I'm not going to go back to fearing you." He blinked, his hand shaking.

"Don't be stupid," she said. But the man with one eye *was* stupid. Tired, sick and stupid. He stood up, still pointing the gun at her as he swayed.

"FIVE YEARS!" he screamed. "Fear, nightmares, anxiety! My woman left me, I have no friends, I couldn't come home! I wish I'd never set foot in your dirt patch of a village, never laid eyes on you and your family! Why couldn't you just *die*, too!?"

Sankofa could have talked him into putting the gun down. He was practically delirious with malaria fever and she certainly knew how that was. Nevertheless, she was glowing and he was falling before he even pulled the trigger. She let the full range of her light fill the room. Anything that was alive would be dead, except Movenpick who stood outside, waiting.

She hadn't realized the depth of her fury until he had answered the door. Her heartrate had not increased, she had not begun to sweat or even think violent thoughts. But the moment she stepped into the house, she knew one thing for sure: She was going to take this man's life. This man had looked up at her in that tree, scoffed at her and gone inside and taken what was hers, leading to the death of everything for her and this life of wandering and wandering, her parents dead. Her brother dead. Her entire town dead. She unleashed it and he burned. Skin, fat, muscle, blood, bile, lymph, finally bone. Nothing but a rib was left when she pulled her light back in.

As the mysterious wind blew his ashes around the living room, the rib tumbled to her feet like an offering. She stared at it. Then she sat on his couch. The rib was clean of meat, a dull yellow, old already. Never had she killed a man out of rage. She got up. She sat down. She stared at the rib. She got up. She left.

Sankofa sniveled, walking past the man's two dead vehicles, her chin pressed to her chest. Movenpick joined her, trotting at her heels, knowing to stay out of her line of vision but in her line of thought. An invisible comfort as always. She was glad. As she walked up the paved road, she shut her eyes and searched, feeling and seeing the green light beneath her eyelids. There. Her seed in the box wasn't far. It was so close that it seemed to toy with her to come, come, COME. It might have been in one of this town's local markets. Maybe being sold as some juju object or piece of junk. With the one-eyed man who'd kept it for years dead, who would know or care what it was but her?

However, Sankofa decided not to follow the internal radar that had been guiding her for years. She walked in the exact opposite direction. And that direction led her to a road and she walked down that road. She walked for days.

"Let it rot in hell," she muttered to herself over those days like a mantra. "Evil thing will not take me with it."

ankofa's leather sandals slapped her heels softly as she walked. Her small swift steps with small swift feet led her to RoboTown.

It was a tiny town, but to Sankofa's eyes it was huge and monstrous like she imagined the Nigerian city of Lagos. She had been walking the Northern region, going from village to village, town to town, spending a few months here, a few weeks there. By this time, she had started specifically asking for and wearing her mother's style of clothes, elaborate outfits made of beautiful stiff wax cloth. Seamstresses often made them specifically for her.

They'd put the clothes aside and keep them until news came that Sankofa was coming through. These seamstresses were always able to locate where to deliver the clothes and, for this reason, they were the heroes of their villages and towns. Sankofa arrived at the crossroads of the northern entrance to RoboTown.

She turned around to see if Movenpick were still trailing her, but he was gone. He always seemed to instinctively know when to make himself scarce.

She paused on the side of the mildly busy road and stared at it for several moments, her mind trying to place what she was observing. It was night and the lights built around the giant silver robot illuminated it like an alien. A real and functioning robot, not just a decoration. As people walked and drove up and down the street, the robot moved its head this way and that, monitoring people. And it spoke instructions in Twi using a firm amplified mildly female voice.

"Put your mobile phone away while you cross, sir."

"I have sent you the directions you need, ma'am. Please, check your mobile device."

"It is safe to cross, ma'am."

The robot was over nine feet tall, appeared to be made of solid steel and had a solar panel and short antennae on top of its head. Broad chested and straight hipped, its shape quite male, despite its feminine voice. Above its head were three large hovering bat-like objects. Drones. The robot stiffly motioned with its expansive arms for traffic on Sankofa's side of the road to move and the other side to stop, its eyes flashing green.

This was the third one of these that she'd seen since leaving home, but this was the first she'd seen that was fully functioning. They were called "robocops" and they were supposedly artificially intelligent. If anything, she was sure they at least were connected to the internet and could scan and search every person around it for information.

As if to prove this, the robocop turned to her as she stood there. It was probably scanning her for any kind of tech so that it could digitally send her a "Welcome to RoboTown" message. How would it react when it realized she didn't even carry a charity mobile? As she walked along the side of the road, following a group of chatty men, one of the robocop's drones flew overhead, black and beetle-like.

"It is safe to cross, kind sirs and young lady," the robocop said, holding up a large metal three-fingered hand and flashing its eyes red at all traffic. As Sankofa passed it with the others, it turned and watched her. Her, not the others. The drone still hovered directly overhead. Her neck prickled, but she moved as if she belonged there. *I am Sankofa, I belong wherever I want to belong*, she thought to herself, walking with her chin up and back straight. She'd been curious about RoboTown for a while and she would satisfy her curiosity starting tonight.

Once across the street, the drones returned to the robocop. As she walked toward the busier part of the town, Sankofa chanced a look over her shoulder. The robot was still watching her, as it conducted traffic.

It was early evening when Sankofa strolled into the market, so it was still open. One section was especially active and well lit, the one where electronics were sold. There were lines and crowds here. Various booths and small shops sold accessories, connection links, and various devices like personal windows, magnetic earbuds, jelli tellis, mobiles.

There was a festive vibe and Sankofa wondered if it was like this every night. Hawkers came to feed the people standing in lines or who'd just bought their items. Friends met up with friends. The excitement was infectious and Sankofa found herself smiling. She slowly ambled along, grasping her satchel, listening and watching. People were too busy looking at blinking glowing shining things to notice her and this was a joy in itself.

However, eventually someone did recognize her and . . . then there was nearly chaos. First there was pointing. Then women selling the electronics rushed and stood protectively in front of their booths as Sankofa passed. Those who were hand-selling cheap mobiles, tablets, windows, clutched their goods and scrambled away from her. One man tripped over his

own feet, dropping his armful of chargers and batteries. He got to his knees right there in the dirt and
snatched up his tangle of chargers and plugs and as
many of the flat black batteries as he could and then
ran off. People knew exactly who she was, which
meant they knew that her presence destroyed tech.
But they didn't know enough to know that it was only
destroyed when she touched it.

Sankofa came to a large shop embedded in a tall red-
brick building. It was called Mr. Starlit Electronics
and there was a line coming out of it so long that it
wrapped around the building three times. Those in
front of the line looked exhausted, sitting on the ground
with food packages and opened bottles of water.

A woman in a bright red sundress stood to the side of
the line smoking a cigarette. Sankofa and the woman
noticed each other at the same time. The woman took
another puff from her cigarette and narrowed her eyes.
Sankofa clutched her satchel and eyed the woman right
back. Her observant eye reminded Sankofa of the robocop. A ripple of murmurs flew through the line as Sankofa passed the shop.

"Girl!"

Sankofa stopped beside an electronics repair booth.
The two women in the booth had already retreated
inside, cowering like bush rats. Sankofa was glad to

have a reason to turn away from them. "Yes?" she said to the smoking woman, curious about her lack of fear.

The woman motioned for Sankofa to come back and Sankofa obliged. A few of the people in line rushed off, but most, though clearly terrified, kept their precious spots. Sankofa stepped up to the woman and the woman smiled at her. For several moments, the two gazed at each other. She was a tall big woman and both of her arms were heavily tattooed. Sankofa had seen plenty of women with tattoos, they had things like hearts, boyfriends' names, sexy animals, symbols chosen by local juju men. Never had she seen anyone, woman or man, with tattoos of circuitry. Just like the insides and parts of computers she saw sold in every market she passed through. This woman had them running up both her arms like a disease.

"You're smaller than I imagined you," she said with a smirk. She took a puff from her cigarette and exhaled the smoke. It smelled sweet and heady. This was the type of cigarette that made people see God, slowed time and attracted happiness.

"Maybe your imagination is not big enough," Sankofa said. "Is this your shop?"

The woman blinked and then her smile grew wider. "I think you are the first person in a long time to ask me that. Most people ask for 'Mr. Starlit.'"

"Well, who *is* Mr. Starlit?"

"An idea born from fear," she said. "I was too afraid to call it *Mrs.* Starlit. That was a long time ago, though."

"Why did you call me over?" Sankofa asked.

The woman crossed her arms over her chest, inspecting Sankofa as if she were the daughter of her best friend. "I like to look into the eyes of hurricanes," she said. She looked around and then said, "Come. I know the routine with you. I'll make you dinner." Then she turned and walked past the line to the store's front door.

People in line gawked at Sankofa as she followed the woman. One man even grabbed the woman's arm and whispered something in her ear as he stared at Sankofa. "I know exactly who she is," the woman snapped in English. She switched back to Twi, "Relax and mind your business." Then she turned to Sankofa, took her hand and said, "Move quickly," as she pulled Sankofa into her shop. Sankofa looked back at people in line just in time to see a man sneer at her. However, no one else left the line. There were jelli tellis stretched across the wall showing the clearest 3D films she'd ever seen, pocket windows on display pedestals, colorful air plugs and other electronic gear; her shop was packed. American music played and the store smelled like the sweat of its anxious customers.

Sankofa walked past all this, holding the woman's

hand. They walked through another door and emerged in back of the building. Here, more people milled around. These ones wore suits and ties. The women wore American-style dresses and pants, too much makeup and fake-looking long-haired weaves with those blue glowing tubes Sankofa saw women in commercials wearing. And it was clear that many of the women flash-bleached their skin, a practice that Sankofa, someone who glowed a dangerous green every so often, could never understand. There were about thirty of them and they all stopped talking when they saw the woman holding Sankofa's hand. When they noticed Sankofa, the whispering began.

"Alhaja," one man said, stepping forward. He carried a glass of what looked like beer and wore a tan suit that looked cartoonish in its perfection. "Do you know who that is??"

"Yes," the woman said. "Mind your business."

She smiled at them all as she led Sankofa to another backdoor and then up some stairs. The stairway was narrow, but the walls were painted white and the air in here was cool and smelled like the inside of a mosque.

"My name's Alhaja Ujala," she said over her shoulder. "You can simply call me Alhaja."

They ascended four flights of stairs, then Alhaja opened a door. Sankofa had been feeling a bit nervous.

She didn't like being in buildings surrounded by what could turn into a mob. Plus, the place was two floors off the ground. Not that anyone could harm her. She just didn't like feeling trapped. When the woman opened the door, she forgot her misgivings.

Mosque-scented air wafted out in a cool plume, giving way to a high-ceilinged blue room. Blue as the morning sky back home. A jelli telli was stretched across the entire wall on the left side of the room. Sankofa stumbled back, hesitant to enter. The woman laughed. "You have sharp senses."

"Isn't that what you expect from the one guarded by the Angel of Death?" Sankofa said, staring at the wall covered with faces. Masks. Ceremonial masks. At least thirty of them. "What is this? Are you a cultist?"

"I'm a *collector*," Alhaja said with a chuckle. "I read a book when I was a child where an old witch had a wall full of these. They would smile, frown, make faces. I always loved that. And I also wanted to grow old and wise like that woman, so you see?"

Sankofa frowned, still skeptical. "So . . . where are they from? What do they do?"

Alhaja shrugged. "I don't know."

Carefully, Sankofa entered the woman's home. "So you're used to bringing things you don't understand into your home."

A large window took up two thirds of the far wall. Sankofa went to it and looked at the crowd outside.

"You've arrived on the busiest day of the year," Alhaja said, stepping up beside her. "And the most dangerous."

"Dangerous?"

"Mine is the only shop that gets the first shipment of the latest models of jelli tellis and portable devices in all of Ghana. And it arrives tonight."

"Ooooh," Sankofa said, understanding why the woman had so happily brought her here. In her first year on her own, a bicycle seller had asked her to stay with his family for two nights to scare away thieves who'd been circling his shop for days. It had worked. "Why here and not Accra or someplace bigger?"

"Because it gives the whole practice some mystery," Alhaja said. "They leak it on the internet and only the most ambitious leave Accra and sometimes as far as places like Lagos, to come here. Want some orange Fanta? Something to eat?"

"I would."

"Come," Alhaja said.

Sankofa sat at the lovely blue wooden dinner table and ate from a blue plate and drank Fanta from a tall blue glass. Alhaja sat across from her the entire time, taking the occasional call on her mobile. She got off the phone and answered the question Sankofa asked minutes ago, "My second husband won the Visa Lottery to America and, instead of taking me, left with a woman willing to give him half a million cedi."

"Oh my goodness!" Sankofa said as she ate her last piece of goat meat. "But . . . why don't you just find another husband?"

"You see how old I am," Alhaja exclaimed with a laugh. "What man will marry me?"

"A smart one," Sankofa said, biting into a slice of fried plantain.

Alhaja threw her head back and laughed heartily. Sankofa snickered. Alhaja's mobile beeped and she tapped the earpiece in her left ear. After a moment, her face grew gravely serious. She looked at Sankofa as she spoke, "When?" She nodded, picking up the mobile and rubbing a finger on the surface. The face of a young dark-skinned man appeared, the focal point of the camera falling on his wide-nostriled nose. He wore a green veil and seemed to be in a moving vehicle that was driving over a rough terrain.

"They won't know when we come, Alhaja, don't worry." He smiled. "And everything is traceable and locked. Even if stolen, no one can use them."

Alhaja sucked her teeth and dismissively waved a hand. "You don't know what these young hackers and rippers are capable of. How far are you?"

"We'll be there in an hour," he said. "Stay outside and wait. I'll flash you."

When she hung up, she leaned against the table. "Sankofa, why don't you get some rest."

She showed Sankofa into another blue room just beside the kitchen. "My daughter's old room," she said, stepping aside. "She's in Singapore working on her master's degree in thermodynamics. She won't mind." Everything in the room, the walls, bed sheets, dresser, table, was a light shade of blue. Sankofa slowly entered, looking up at the high ceiling, which was like the afternoon sky.

"Pretty," she whispered. Just standing in the room made her feel at peace.

"How old are you?" Alhaja asked.

Sankofa nearly gave her usual answer, which was, "How old do I look?" But she caught herself. Alhaja wasn't just anyone. "Thirteen," she said. Then she gazed into Alhaja's eyes and waited. People always had something to say about her age.

"Old enough for honesty," Alhaja said. "You look younger than that but I know you're older than your years, so I'll be upfront. I need you."

A smile spread across Sankofa's face and she laughed. "I know. I've done this before. Fear of death is a powerful weapon." This was a line from a book she'd once read whose title she'd long since forgotten.

"They'll come with guns," Alhaja said. "They've already sent us a text warning of their coming and instructed me on where to leave the merchandise so that no one is killed. They're bold."

"Oh," Sankofa exclaimed. "Have they come before?"

"Other towns, never here," she said. "They call themselves the Bandit Boys."

Sankofa walked to the bed and eyed its blue sheets. She sat down and ran a hand over the surface. Soft and cool. She slipped off her sandals and said, "One hour?"

"About that."

"Will you wake me up when they come?"

Alhaja smiled, but her eyes were hard. "Definitely."

Sankofa was lying in the forest on a bed of grass and leaves, glad to be alone back in the wilderness, again, with the fruits and trees and Movenpick skulking nearby. She was completely at peace, no pull from the evil seed in the box. But someone was shaking her. She curled herself tighter and then she awoke. Sky blue. Sky blue ceiling.

"Oh," she said, looking wildly into Alhaja's eyes. "They're here?"

Alhaja handed her a cup of hot coffee. "Come."

Sankofa slipped her sandals on, took the cup and looked into it. Something fluttered in her chest and she shut her eyes. On the surface was the pull of the seed, which she ignored easily. *Nothing* could make her return to that search. But beneath that feeling was a yearning for the forest, again. The quiet, the escape. She sniffed the coffee and the smell brought with it a very clear image of her father. He loved coffee and her mother made it for him every morning. The smell would permeate the house and she and her brother would always come to sniff it, but their father would never ever let them taste the coffee. Her father hadn't been a tall or muscular man. She'd encountered many tall muscular men since leaving home; she knew them well. Her father was slight, and kind, and gentle and he loved coffee, prayer and cigarettes.

"This is a man's beverage," he'd simply said. Then he'd bring up the cup, sniff the aroma, smile to himself, take a sip and sit back and sigh, "Aaaaaah, that's good coffee."

Sankofa put the cup down without taking a sip and followed Alhaja out of the room.

As she stepped outside where the group of wealthy

folk had been gathered, she saw the truck. It was an ugly broken-down piece of machinery and she doubted if her technology-killing touch would have much of an effect on it. Its outer shell was crusted with rust, the headlights were broken, and its engine was exposed; it looked as if it had been cobbled together from the parts of already ancient damaged vehicles.

Its trunk was full of oranges. At least on the surface. Alhaja took Sankofa's arm. "They'll come to the storefront. The better to make a spectacle that everyone will talk about."

In front, the line was so long that Sankofa couldn't see the end of it. Beside the line was a crowd of curious onlookers.

"Is it always like this?" she asked.

"Yes," Alhaja said, lighting one of her special cigarettes. She was looking around as if she expected monsters to burst from between the nearby market booths and alleys. Sankofa frowned, and started looking around, too. And that was how she was the first to spot the group of men in red. She blinked for a moment then tapped Alhaja's shoulder. When Alhaja looked at her, Sankofa pointed.

"Oh shit," Alhaja muttered, the cigarette dangling between her lips.

One of the men in red stepped forward, separating

himself from the crowd. He was grinning, his teeth shining brightly in the store's light. He had wild long hair, dreadlocks. Sankofa had never seen such hair in real life, but she'd seen it plenty in the movies she watched back home when they had public jelli telli nights near the mosque. It looked even more spectacular up close and in real life.

He didn't speak, clearly waiting for everyone in the line to see him. Many brought out mobile phones and windows to take pictures of him. He pointed at Alhaja and nodded. "Mrs. Starlit. Chalé, how easy you go make this for yourself?" he said in English.

"Go home," Alhaja said in Twi.

"No hired guns," he said in English. He switched back to Twi. "Didn't we tell you we were coming? Maybe you're as smart as you look, Mrs. Starlit."

"I told my gunmen to stay home," she said. "I don't need them today."

Now others pushed through the crowd of onlookers, standing beside the line of customers, directly in front of Alhaja. There were at least ten of them. They carried guns, machetes, batons, cudgels. Wild haired. And smiling. Sankofa glanced at the people in the line and she knew this was a moment of choice. She'd been at the center of this kind of thing before. The people would flee and Alhaja would lose both her customers and merchandise. And maybe a few people would die, too.

"You're just a woman," the one with the longest dreadlocks said. "So do what women do, step back and let us take."

The others laughed and none of them took a step forward or backwards.

"Maybe you are thinking of your own failed mother," Alhaja snapped. "If you want something, you'll have to buy it. My favorite is the upgraded jelli telli. The gel is stretchier, it smells like flowers instead of chemicals, the picture and sound make you feel like you're right in the movie. And it holds up better in the heat." Sankofa was looking at Alhaja's back, but she could tell from her tone that she was smirking, trying so hard to look arrogant and sure.

"Get off my property," Alhaja suddenly sneered. "You're scaring my customers."

It happened too fast. Sankofa was standing behind her. Everyone was watching. The cudgel flew like a swooping bird. She saw it in slow motion and as she watched the wooden object sail, she noticed something else. A glint in the sky. A drone. Right above them all. And then the round and hardest part of the cudgel hit Alhaja on the arm and she fell down.

Sankofa's eyes locked on the men in red as they started to rush forward, their legs bending, sandaled and shoed feet grinding into the dirt, weight shifting forward. Sankofa stepped over the fallen Alhaja and became the moon.

Everyone ran.

Good, she thought, relieved. The fear was what she'd relied on. She couldn't control her light enough not to kill many in the area, so she wasn't about to try and target any of the thieves as they ran.

The people in line, the men in red, everyone fled, except Alhaja. Sankofa smiled in the silence and dust rising from all the scrambling feet. She looked up. The drone was still there. She grunted and helped Alhaja to her feet.

Alhaja's customers returned the next day. The men in red did not. Alhaja stood outside from sun up to sun down as people came and bought just about every unit of new product she had, a bandage on her arm and Sankofa standing beside her. People came from farther away, flying in, driving in, by bus, kabu kabu, all to buy new tech. And to see Sankofa. The news of what happened spread fast and far within minutes. By the end of the day there was reason for all of Alhaja's employees and friends to hold an impromptu party. Sankofa retreated to her bed, exhausted.

She'd done little else all day but stand around looking as menacing as she could muster. However, Sankofa had a lot on her mind. She'd saved Alhaja's shop from armed robbers, but all she could think of was her father. The smell of that coffee. She wanted everyone to leave her be, including Alhaja. She had done what Alhaja needed done and she didn't want to celebrate, explain herself, or be stared at. She considered leaving in the dead of night, but instead lay in that comfortable soft blue bed and pushed her face to the sheet and let her tears run. For hours. Because of the scent of coffee she remembered that she wanted her father. And he was dead. Because she'd killed him.

When she was finally able to drag herself out of bed, it was dark outside and the shop was quiet. She found Alhaja in the kitchen, sitting at the table sipping a cup of tea. She looked up at Sankofa and cocked her head. "Do you want something to eat?"

That was all. No questions, no demands. It was so nice. She and Alhaja never discussed it. They never planned for it. It just happened. Sankofa moved in to that room, setting her satchel on the dresser and lying on the bed and looking up at the blue ceiling. When the sun came up the second day, the room lit up like the sky. Sankofa shut her eyes, enjoying the warmth of the light on her skin.

On her third day in RoboTown, Alhaja walked with Sankofa to the local mosque. The walk there took a half hour. "This way, I can also show you much of RoboTown," she said. "Best way to learn it is on foot."

"It's the only way I can learn it," Sankofa said.

"Oh, that's right, you can't ride in cars." She looked at Sankofa, frowning. "Why is that?"

Sankofa shrugged and asked, "Why do I glow?"

Alhaja nodded. "True. Mysteries are a mystery. Also, maybe if people see you walking, they'll stop being afraid."

"People are always afraid of me. For good reason."

"Maybe if you didn't go around reminding everyone by glowing in public, that might change," Alhaja gently said.

Sankofa smiled. Yesterday morning when she'd gone outside to look at the avocado tree in the backyard, mosquitoes had tried to make a meal of her as they often did. She'd responded in her usual way, by glowing a little bit to kill them off and deter the living ones. A small group of women happened to have been passing by and they saw her do this. By afternoon, an even larger group of women had come to Alhaja's home and, regardless of the fact that Sankofa was in her room close enough to hear, told Alhaja to get rid of her. Sankofa was glad they didn't notice Movenpick perched in the branches amongst the unripe avocados.

So Alhaja is ok with me using my glow to save her shop, but not with me using it to save my own blood, Sankofa thought. Yes, to her, people were strange. Sankofa may have forgotten her name, but she remembered those early days of malaria, when she'd lain in bed shuddering, her body throbbing with the drum beat of deep aches, where it felt as if lightning were shooting through her legs, where she felt as if she were being repeatedly stung all over her body by giant mosquitoes. Over and over, this disease attacked her body . . . until the day the tree offered her the box. Let the women of RoboTown gossip, let Alhaja feel mildly uncomfortable; Sankofa's hatred of mosquitoes was purely justified and she would keep zapping them with her light when she so pleased.

Still, Sankofa was looking forward to going to the mosque. She hadn't been inside one since the day she'd killed her home. She vividly remembered seeing her father there, dead with all the other men. The silence in a place that had always been filled with the sound of prayer. She'd brought death in there. Always in the back of her mind, though she was still alive and healthy, she'd wondered if Allah was angry with her.

The mosque was a small grey building. There were no flourishes on the outside, and there was no Arabic script anywhere, except above the entrance. The place looked nothing like the mosque back home. *It's still a house of Allah,* she reminded herself. Waiting at the entrance was a fat woman with smooth dark brown skin. She wore a grey wide dress that probably was making her look even fatter and a black hijab around her head. Her fatness made it difficult to tell how old she was.

"Sister Kumi," Alhaja said, giving the woman a hug.

"Alhaja," she said. Then she turned to Sankofa with a kind smile. "Sankofa," she breathed. "It's an honor to meet a legend. Please come in."

When Alhaja pushed her toward Sister Kumi and then did not follow, she looked at her with question. "I'll be back for you in an hour," Alhaja said.

Sister Kumi led Sankofa to a small room in the back of the modest mosque. There were several overlapping oriental rugs covering the floor and a tea set in the corner with hot tea already poured into the tiny cups.

"Sit," she said. "This is my meeting room. Make yourself comfortable. I can bring chairs if you like, but something told me you'd prefer the floor."

Sankofa wanted to be offended. Did she think she

was some kind of animal or bush girl? But the woman was right, Sankofa *did* prefer the floor, and she *had* spent a week in the bush once and loved it so much that she yearned to return to it. So she sat down on the floor and crossed her short legs. With far more effort, Sister Kumi did the same, though she simply sat with her thick legs stretched before her.

They stared at each other, Sister Kumi still breathing heavily from the exertion of sitting down. Sankofa was not afraid to look into people's eyes, but usually they were afraid to look into hers. Not Sister Kumi, she seemed perfectly fine, gazing into Sankofa's eyes. They looked into each other's eyes for so long that Sankofa could see that Sister Kumi's dark brown eyes curved down at their edges and she had two small discolorations on the white of her right eye.

"I see it, even when you don't make it happen," Sister Kumi said after a while.

Sankofa nodded. "Most don't because they're afraid to look for too long, but it's always there."

"The evil."

"I don't know it to be evil. Not what's in me."

"It brings death."

"Only when I want it to. Everything dies, animals, plants, things . . ." She trailed off because Sister Kumi was just staring at her again.

"Why'd you come to RoboTown?"

Sankofa shrugged. "It was in the opposite direction."

"From where?"

"Evil."

"I've heard the stories about you and quite frankly, I am shocked to be here sitting with you. A part of me wants to deny it's really you. Alhaja and several others talked about what they saw two nights ago and I see what I see in your eyes but . . . my heart is still denying."

"I could show you if you want."

"Where are your parents?"

"Dead."

"Because of you?"

Sankofa frowned at her.

"Do you believe in Allah?"

"Yes," Sankofa said.

Sister Kumi smiled glowingly and breathed a sigh of relief. "Good. Because I was about to say that even a djinn can be converted."

Sankofa frowned, irritably thinking, *I'm not a djinn*. She pushed away her annoyance because she had questions. "Why did Allah make me this way? What did I do?" She thought of the seed in the box and how her father had sold it off without a thought, how the politician had died soon after buying it, and how the abilities the seed gave her seemed to have corrupted in its absence. For the millionth time, she wondered if Allah had wanted her to fight harder for it. To stand up to the politician and even her father. But who stood up to one's father?

"Sometimes we have evil inside us and only Allah knows why," Sister Kumi said. She leaned forward. "So to control your . . . death light last night, you had to push your emotions down deep? Is that how you control it?" Sister Kumi said, pressing the fingers of her right hand to the center of her chest.

"Maybe," Sankofa said. "I don't know if—"

"Maybe if you press the urge to *glow* down deep and hard enough, you can smother it, put it out."

"I . . . I can try," Sankofa said, unsure. A tantalizing idea crossed her mind like a colorful bird . . . *Maybe I* can *return to normal.* She considered just forgetting about the seed in a box and she felt an immense weight lift from her shoulders. And with that weight went the burden of guilt she felt for the deaths of her family and town. She would not just bury those memories, she would leave that entire grave behind. *I'll stay in RoboTown with Alhaja and be normal.* She took in a sharp breath and grinned. Sister Kumi reached forward and took her hand.

"Let us recite the ninety-nine names of Allah," she said. "Just repeat after me if you don't know them."

Sankofa nodded. She'd never heard of such a thing.

"And from today forth, you will wear a hijab. You're young, but you've been through things that put you far beyond your years. You must cover up. We will cure you, yet."

After naming Allah ninety-nine times, for the next hour, they prayed familiar words that brought Sankofa right back to the mosque in Wulugu. When her parents and her town were still alive. When she and her brother used to fight and play in the house. When she climbed the shea tree and the earth had yet to offer her the box. The more she spoke the words of the Quran, the harder she pushed those memories down within her, imagining them pressing the strange light in her to the ground, smothering it until it went out. When they both looked up, Sankofa hugged Sister Kumi tightly and the woman's folds of fat were like the embrace of Allah. She'd never forget her family. She loved her family, would always be part of it. But she would be normal; let the seed in the box go. Yes. Here was a chance.

When Alhaja came for her late that afternoon, Sankofa was wearing a grey hijab over her short-haired wig and a smile on her face.

CHAPTER 8

EVERYTHING HAPPENS IN THE MARKET

Sankofa quickly learned that the citizens of RoboTown cherished their robocop, and this made it one of very few robocops in Ghana to not be vandalized, stolen or hacked into. The people of RoboTown guarded their street robot with such care that it might as well have been one of their most prized citizens. A crew polished it every week, scrubbing every nook and cranny with a special solution made by one of the town's old women and thus the robot shined immaculately for most of the week when there wasn't rain. Sankofa learned that on the day she'd arrived, it had rained for two days before. Otherwise, she'd have been greeted that day by a shining robocop that practically glowed in the dark.

Sankofa went to look at it after the incident at Mr. Starlit. As it had when she first entered RoboTown, it paid special attention to her, turning its head to watch her the entire time that she was there. "Don't worry," Alhaja had told her when Sankofa mentioned it to her later. "It's only because you have nothing on you that it can scan. It's like a nosy old woman when she's denied gossip."

The robocop's drone also liked to follow Sankofa around and this was quite annoying. What was even more annoying was the fact that Sankofa couldn't study the robocop on the internet or in eBooks because tech died at her touch. All she could do was ask questions of whomever had knowledge—old-fashioned research. Alhaja knew much about the robocop, but the youth of RoboTown knew even more. They had time to do research and they were most interested in the information because the more they knew, the more they could get away with mischief, like having flash parties.

RoboTown was a somewhat strict Islamic town and parties were frowned upon. However, RoboTown youth always found a way. Sankofa's general reputation and the incident at Mr. Starlit earned her respect from the older teens, so they were more than happy to answer her questions. Thus, she learned from these older kids that the drones were the mobile eyes of the robocop.

"They stay high up because we knock them down when they're stupid enough to get too close," one boy told Sankofa. "We leave them, though. They have trackers. Not worth the trouble. They don't follow you for very long, anyway."

Sankofa frowned. One of the robocop's drones had been following her for months. "What's the point of them?" she asked. "Are they looking for troublemakers? Who's collecting all the data? And who repairs the ones you've broken?"

All the boys in the group laughed. Sankofa simply waited.

"Everything's collecting data," one of the boys said. His name was Michael and he was always asking Sankofa to attend the flash parties he liked to organize. "All these devices we use are spies. That's why you're like a superhero; they can't control you. You wearing hijab now must drive the spies crazy because they can't easily see your face."

Several of the boys agreed.

"The thing has its own agenda," Michael said, lighting a cigarette. "And it takes care of itself."

"What does that mean?" she asked.

"Na artificially intelligent," Michael said in pidgin English, blowing out a mouthful of smoke. He switched back to Twi, "No man behind the curtain anymore."

"It's a demon. Abomination," one of the other boys declared, and they all started laughing and slapping hands in agreement.

Alhaja told Sankofa the robot had been there for decades and that before its arrival that traffic intersection
had been rife with death. Car collisions, pedestrians
constantly being struck and killed, road rage incidents
and even late-night robberies. She didn't know whose
idea the robot was but things changed as soon as it was
installed. People were intrigued by the robot and when
national newspapers started coming to do stories about
it, they grew proud of it. Commerce increased and RoboTown became more affluent. And with this pride
came a respect and an affection for the robot.

"It was interesting," Alhaja said. "People treat it
with more respect than they treat any police officer.
Maybe because the robot is polite, helpful and never
asks for bribes." She'd laughed and then leaned in
with a conspiratorial smirk. "The thing answers to
no one now, but do you know who programmed it ini-
tially? Sister Kumi."

"What?" Sankofa exclaimed.

Alhaja nodded. "Before she married and became
the Imam's wife, she was an electrical engineer and in
charge of the local Robocop Project."

In Sankofa's years on the road, she'd learned that
people were complicated. They wore masks and
guises to protect or hide their real selves. They re-
invented themselves. They destroyed themselves.

They built on themselves. She understood people and their often contradictory ways, but that robo-cop was not a person.

Sankofa was in the market.

The avocado tree's fruit were all finally ready for picking and over the last week, Sankofa had climbed into the tree and carefully picked every single one. Movenpick hadn't been there and she'd vaguely wondered where he'd gone. Most likely he'd snuck into the nearby trees to forage, as usual. Alhaja had then sent out a mass text alerting the women and each had made an appointment to come and buy some. Sankofa got to choose and eat one of the avocados; experiencing its rich buttery goodness made it clear to her why there was so much competition to buy one of Alhaja's avocados.

Once they were all sold, Alhaja gave Sankofa a third of the money to spend on herself. Sankofa was stunned. This was more money than she'd ever had for herself in her entire life and she'd meticulously folded the bills and put them in the deep pocket of her dress. She went to the market.

She was walking through the section where sellers sold textiles. The selection today was wonderfully colorful. A new seller must have come and the place was full of jostling women. When they saw her, they made room, but continued with their negotiations. She looked around some, pulling her grey hijab back for a better look around. Today, she had enough money to buy ten pieces of beautiful cloth if she wanted and *still* afford to have them sewn into dresses to fit her small frame.

She was passing the edge of the new seller's table when she saw it. She stopped, women moving around her toward the main section of the large booth to grab and inspect the textiles. On this side of the table were several miscellaneous things. A mysterious hand-sized cube covered with circuitry and loose wires that looked like it had been pulled right out of a machine. A small wooden figurine of a large-breasted woman that looked like it had been rubbed so many times that it was losing its shape. A sleek black drone that looked like an insect.

And a wooden box.

For several moments, Sankofa just stood there feeling faint. She breathed through her mouth. Was this a dream? Or more likely, a nightmare? She went to it. She felt cold, her muscles stiff. Her head was pounding now. She had buried the internal GPS for it deep down, so deep that she'd nearly forgotten it. She'd let it be lost; she had let go. And because of that, the goddamn, evil, vindictive, life-destroying thing had decided to change tactics and find *her*.

It looked the same. Oh it looked exactly the same. "Oh my God," she whispered, now looking down at it. She reached out to pick it up.

"Hey," a man snapped. "What are you doing?"

Her heart was beating so fast. It was all she had left of home . . . and she wanted to crush the thing right then and there. She stammered, "I . . . I was going to . . ."

"Nothing here is for your hands," he said.

Go away, sir. This is none of your business, she darkly thought, staring at the box.

The man turned to look at a woman holding up a red and yellow sheet of textile calling for him. "Just wait," he said. "I'm coming."

"How much?" Sankofa asked. "Please."

"You can *never* afford it. These things are for Big Men with Big Money."

Sankofa stared at the man. "Says who?"

"Child, leave here, you're wasting my time."

She stepped closer and cocked her head, her heart thumping faster. "Do you know who I am?" she asked in a low voice. There was no way in hell she was going anywhere.

"Yes, you're a girl who is wasting my time and about to be slapped," he said, raising a hand. "Get out of here."

She stepped closer to the table, closer to the man,

locking eyes with him. Angry. Oh, she would have this box, one way or another. If he tried to take the box away, there would be death today. She brought her light to her face, feeling it warm the skin of her cheeks. He was close enough to see it rush forward from deep in her flesh, like a hidden spirit deciding to show itself. When she saw his eyes widen and start watering, she smiled. He pushed the box toward her. "Take it."

"Where did you get it?" she asked.

"Another seller, who got it from another seller, who got it from some guy," he gibbered. "It's one of those things that's sold, stolen, found, sold, so on. Someone said it even belonged to the Minister of Finance, you know the Man of the Gold Shoe? I-I don't know what it is. Just. . . . just some useless thing."

Sankofa reached into her pocket for her wad of bills. She held it up and split it in half. She slapped half on the table in front of the man. "I will pay for it," she said. She put the rest back in her pocket.

"Oh. My. Wow. Thank you, Ma'am," he said, looking at the money, then at her and then back at the money. "I wouldn't have sold it for this much to even a Big Man. You don't have to—"

"Stop talking and be grateful," she said, taking the box. Yes, this was the box. She knew it as soon as her hands touched it. The wood of the shea tree from home. The smell of it. The pull of it. Her hand fell on it more heavily than she meant it to. It seemed smaller than she remembered, but then again, she'd last seen it years ago, when *she* was smaller. Sankofa turned away and walked out of the textile section into the place where they were selling vegetables. She turned to one of the wooden dividers and held up the box. Slowly, she opened it. There it was. *A seed is actually a lot like an egg,* she thought. She quickly shut it, feeling the rush of tears cloud her vision. She leaned her head against the wooden divider and exhaled.

Sankofa bought some fried plantain and kenkey and walked to a quiet spot between two trees to sit and eat. Shutting her eyes, she spoke a prayer to Allah. She touched the box deep in her pocket, the one not heavy with the rest of her money and sighed. Could it even be destroyed? She brought out her jar of shea butter and rubbed some on her hands and neck. She cupped her hands to her nose and inhaled the nutty scent. She leaned back against the tree trunk, pulled her hijab closer to her face, opened the warm foil and pulled a juicy plantain slice from it. Her denial-fueled peace was interrupted by a soft whirring sound.

The palm tree and bush behind her gave some

privacy from the busy market. Privacy where human beings were concerned. Robots were another issue. The drone hovered feet away, this time, at eye level. Sleek, black and insectile. It had four propellers on each side and Sankofa could feel the air from their spinning. It was square shaped with dull angles, glinting in the late afternoon light. The glinting was from its many tiny camera eyes embedded all around its edges. As it hovered, the eyes smoothly rotated this way and that.

All Sankofa wanted in this moment was some privacy. To be away from watchful, curious, judgmental, prying eyes. Just for this little moment. She needed to be still and alone . . . and unwatched. And here this drone was spying on her with its many tiny embedded cameras. She scowled at it and muttered, "Come a little closer, you nosy thing." Her heart was beating fast, the irritation flowing into her blood. For so many months, the drone had been following her, spying from afar. Now, it had grown bold and was disturbing her delicious meal. This was *not* the time.

And still, it came closer. Three feet away, now. Two feet. A foot. Sankofa dropped her slice of plantain and grabbed with both hands, making sure to avoid the propellers. Within a moment, it stopped functioning, dead in her grasp. Sankofa grunted with satisfaction, then she felt a sting of guilt.

"Hey!" a man shouted, stepping closer. He was carrying a large bunch of green plantains on his shoulder. "What have you done?"

Sankofa opened her mouth to speak, but she had no words. What *had* she done?

More people came around the bushes and tree to see. Sankofa threw the drone down, grabbed her food and leapt to her feet. "You see that?" the man was telling another man who'd come running over.

"Eh!" a large woman, carrying several bags said, stepping up. "Sankofa, what . . ."

"I . . . it was in my face," Sankofa said.

"What is that thing?" another woman asked.

"It's one of robocop's eyes," someone said. "Oh my God, it looks dead. She's killed it."

"The thing that flies like alien ship?" someone asked in English.

And that was when they all heard the loud crash from the other side of the market square. From the street. People turned to look and without a word, everyone rushed to see what had happened. Sankofa threw off her hijab, grabbed the drone and took off for Alhaja's house.

As she ran, the world around her blurred from the tears in her eyes and the fact that she could barely breathe. *Why am I carrying this thing?* she vaguely wondered. But her hands wouldn't drop the drone. She passed more people, all running in the other direction. When she arrived at Mr. Starlit, people were just leaving the store.

Alhaja was behind the counter. "Sankofa, what happened? I heard there's been an accident at the intersection! First in decades. Is it true?" She blinked. "Where's your hijab? You can't—" She'd noticed the drone Sankofa carried and her eyes grew large.

Sankofa dashed past her, to the back of the store, out the back and up the stairs. She locked herself in her room and sank to the floor. Suddenly very sleepy, she calmed enough so that her tears stopped and her breathing slowed. Then, for the first time in nearly a year, it rushed into her—her light. She laid down right there on the rug, sighing as it washed into her like heavy warm water, uncontrolled, gradual, loose, free. If there had been anyone, animal or plant, around her, they'd have been dead.

Someone banging on her door jarred her awake.

"Open up," a man's voice said. "Now! Witch."

She slowly opened her eyes, as the banging continued. She was still curled on the floor, cradling the drone. The banging grew harder and then someone tried to open the door. She threw the drone she still carried aside and got to her feet.

"Sankofa," she heard Alhaja say. "My dear, are you there?"

Sankofa ran to her closet and pushed the clothes Alhaja had bought her over the months aside, including the brand-new school uniform Alhaja bought two weeks ago. After nearly a year, the local school had agreed she was safe enough to join her mates in getting an education. Sankofa had really been looking forward to it. She grabbed her green and yellow wrapper and matching top, shrugged out of her pants and T-shirt and put them on.

"We hear you in there," the man said. "Don't make us have to destroy Alhaja's home by breaking down this door. You've done enough da—"

"I'm coming," she said. "Let me dress."

She took her time tying her bright green head wrap. When she finished, Sankofa looked around her blue room with the blue ceiling and the blue soft bed she'd come to love so much. She grabbed her satchel and slung it over her shoulder. By this time, she had noticed the noise of the growing mob outside. Voices and the shuffle of feet.

"So stupid to come here seeking me," Sankofa muttered. She rubbed her face. "I've been here too long."

She opened the door. The five people waiting for her knew not to grab her.

A child had been killed at the intersection. The seven-and-a-half-year-old had been crossing with his mother and two other people. All four people had had mobile phones on them, yes, even the child. Their names were Mary, Akua, Ason and Kweku. They all lived in RoboTown. The robocop had plenty to scan and read on them. None of them were mysteries. Yet at some point as the four of them crossed, the robocop had made a mistake. Some said it had not "been paying attention." Its head was turned toward the market, many said. And as it had looked toward the market, it had shown a green light while it told the people to cross. The man who'd run over the seven-and-a-half-year-old said he had not seen the child.

How did he not see? Sankofa wondered as she followed the Imam, Alhaja by her side, three men following close behind her, and many of RoboTown's citizens noisily following behind them. *Are the robocop's false eyes the only eyes he has?* She grasped her satchel to her, and glanced behind her at the line of police officers keeping everyone back, all armed with automatic guns. She made eye contact with one of them and his look was so nasty that she turned back around. Sankofa took a deep breath.

When she arrived at the intersection, the child was still in the street, his mother weeping over his twisted body. Sankofa looked at this and remembered how she'd gone flying that fateful day. The woman who had to have heard them coming from a half mile away didn't look up or stop sobbing.

"See this poor woman!"

"This is what happens when you bring Death's Daughter to RoboTown."

"We'll deal with her."

"Witch!"

Sankofa shut her eyes, trying to block out the mob's shouting. Being led out of town by an angry mob wasn't the worst thing that could happen, best to stay calm and let it be done. She had all she needed in her satchel. Still, she'd grown to love RoboTown. It may not have been *her* home but for a nearly a year, it had been *a* home. And Alhaja had been so good to her, almost a mother. And Sister Kumi. And Michael and the other kids. And she was going to go to school again.

They passed the sobbing woman and her dead son. They passed the stopped cars and trucks. Many had gotten out and were just staring at the woman. Sankofa thought they'd walk right through the intersection, out of town. Then the Imam stopped in the middle of the intersection, before the robocop.

This was her first time close to it. No one stepped up to the robocop, except its cleaners. It just wasn't polite. Its location was not a spot for pedestrians. Now the busy street was empty, police cordoning off the road. But a mob was gathering. Sankofa looked at the robocop's massive feet, broad torso, and then up at its complex head with eyes shining its "stop" red. Its head made a soft whirring sound as it looked down at her with its stoplight eyes.

"Wife, come," the Imam called loudly over his shoulder.

Sankofa turned around and watched Sister Kumi push her way through the line of police officers. She was breathing heavily, as usual. Today she wore a grey dress and a grey veil over her head. "Why?" she asked Sankofa.

Sankofa sighed and shook her head. "Please, just let me leave RoboTown."

"Ask it," the Imam said. "So we are sure."

Sister Kumi looked from Sankofa to her husband and back to Sankofa. Then she turned to the robocop and held up a tiny black box, a remote control. She spoke into it, "Speak your mind, Steel Brother."

"One has died today on my watch," it said in its sonorous female voice. "At 14:55 hours in Section 4 of the Kumasi Road intersection. A child, Ason Ayim, age 7 and a half. I said walk and gave Section 3 the Green light at the same time. I made a mistake. I am very sorry for your loss."

"What made you make this mistake," Sister Kumi asked, looking right at Sankofa.

The robocop whose name Sankofa now knew was "Steel Brother" paused. It looked at Sankofa, as well. And as it did, its remaining drone came down and hovered feet above their heads. "That one there has no digital footprint. How can one have no digital footprint? No device, no face recognition software can recognize, no voice that responds to my voice recognition software. And that one there, she is . . . that one there, she is . . . that one there, she is . . . ."

Then Steel Brother seemed to freeze, its massive head turned toward Sankofa. Sister Kumi looked at her husband. "What's wrong with it?" the Imam asked.

"I don't know!" Sister Kumi whispered.

"That one there, she is," Steel Brother said, this time more decisively. ". . . Confusion. I experience confusion because of her. I spend memory on that one. I burn my energy stores on that one. Trying to understand. For me to do my job, I have to have information. That one there, she is distracting. I was gathering information on that one and that one took my eyes."

"Your drone?" Sister Kumi asked.

"Yes. And that drew *all* my attention. And I grew confused. And I made my mistake." The robot went silent and there was a moment when Sankofa could hear the crickets in the bushes beside the road. Then everyone in the mob began to speak at once—from name calling, to discussing how a robot could make a mistake, to considering the plight of RoboTown now that its robot was stupid.

All Sankofa could think of was the clear fact that the robocop had become obsessed with her to the point of being distracted enough to cause an accident and maybe it was even driving itself mad.

"Get out of our town!" a woman shrieked. Then the first stone flew past Sankofa's head. "GET OUT!" It was the mother of the dead child. She'd left his corpse, found a large stone, thrown it and was preparing to throw another one. Her wet face was swollen, her eyes red, her nose slick with snot. "BAD LUCK! YOU'RE BAD LUCK! WITCH! EVIL REMOTE CONTROL! SATAN!" She picked up and threw another stone. It hit Sankofa in the leg.

Another stone came from the mob. It zoomed past Sankofa's face. Then the pushing and shoving with the police started. Police fell and people began kicking them. Alhaja grabbed Sankofa's arm and pulled her back, but people quickly surrounded them.

"This woman who thinks she's something because she overcharges us for mobile phones and jelli tellis," a woman sneered. "Of course, she sides with this monster." A stone hit Alhaja and the Imam quickly jumped in front of her.

"People! People of RoboTown," he shouted. "Is this the way to show Allah your excellence?! Is this . . ."

His strong voice was drowned out by the yelling of those around him. Another stone hit Sankofa in the arm and she stumbled back, dropping Alhaja's hand. "Stop it!" she shouted. She could feel her light just beneath her skin. It wanted to defend her, to protect her. *No*, Sankofa thought, squeezing her mouth, flaring her nostrils and frowning. *Alhaja is too close, I can't control it that well . . . and I won't hurt these people of RoboTown. Cannot! Never!* But they were hurting her.

Another stone hit her right on the collarbone. "Ah!" she screamed, bending forward in pain. "Please!" In every direction she looked were people shouting. Every direction except Alhaja's; she met Sankofa's eyes and Sankofa saw such sorrow there. "I'm sorry," Sankofa said. "Oh I'm so sorry."

"Witch," a man said, chucking a stone. It hit her in the thigh. Sankofa screeched, turned the other way, and ran headfirst into the belly of a fat man. He shoved her back and threw dirt at her. "Leave this place," he said.

"You have to *let* me!" Sankofa screamed, tears flying from her eyes. "How can I leave if . . ."

A flip-flop bounced off her head, then more dirt sprayed into her face. Someone slapped her, but she couldn't see who'd done it because her eyes were watering so badly. Someone kicked her in the back and she moaned in pain, her chest hitching as she sobbed "Please! I didn't mean to—" She was punched in the side, and she stumbled the other way, coughing and holding her chest. "See!" someone shouted. "She *can* be cut down! Get her!"

At some point she fell, trying to catch her breath. Someone shoved Alhaja out of the way and they were on her. The blows seemed to rain from the sky and still Sankofa fought to hold it in. She would not harm RoboTown. This was the only home she had. Hot painful water splashing onto her body. She curled herself tightly into a ball. *No,* she thought. *I won't. I can't. Not again.* They only thought of their town's reputation. Maybe it had been too long since they'd seen violence. Or felt a need to respond with it. Had RoboTown been too content? Sankofa didn't know. What she knew was that when the green deadly light burst

from her, it felt like cool water. It put out the flames.
Everything went quiet.

She stayed that way for over a minute. "No, no, no,
why," she whispered, her face pressed to the road. When
she looked to the side, first she saw red fur. Movenpick
stood up now, but didn't move from her side. She sat up,
seeing beyond the fox. She gasped. She was surrounded
by nine or ten dead bodies. She had controlled it. This
she knew. She had only allowed a fraction of the light
to come. But it was enough to cause several around
her to drop dead. There would be bodies left to bury.
Those who still stood, alive, stepped back, mouths
open, words lost, eyes twitching with terror. Sankofa's
eye fell on the fallen body of Alhaja and she shrieked.
Then she ran. People got out of her way.

Sankofa fled up the road, her chest burning and her
nose bleeding. One of her eyes was swelling shut. She
paused after about a half mile and looked back. No
one was following her and from here, she could hear
people beginning to wail as they surrounded the dead.

Then she saw it high in the sky. She was wrong.

One person had followed her. The Steel Brother, the robocop. "I also send reports to LifeGen," it said. Projecting its voice so precisely, even from a distance she could hear its every word clearly.

"LifeGen?" she said. The shock of this made her stumble over her feet. "You've been spying on me for . . . for them?" *Is LifeGen responsible for the seed coming back into my life?* she wondered. The world around her swam. *What did all this mean? Why?*

"You are confusion," it said. "LifeGen studies you. Then it will find use for you." It was so fast that she only managed seven steps before the burst of lightning from the drone's wireless Taser travelled from her head all the way down to her toes. Her last thought was *I thought drones could only do that in the movies.*

Then Sankofa remembered nothing.

CHAPTER 9
DEATH

Whimpering. Someone was whimpering. And tapping her shoulder.

Soil. Rich fragrant soil. She pursed her lips and pressed her tongue to the roof of her mouth, smearing it with a coat of the soil. She worked her jaw and flexed her legs and the muscles of her thighs locked with cramps. The pain of it shot through her body. And someone was still tapping at her shoulder, moving up to her neck. A warm wet roughness rubbed at her cheek.

She cracked open her eyes to a shadow hovering over her. The shadow whimpered, moving back as she sat up. "Mo . . . pick?" she muttered, her mouth too gummy to fully pronounce the name. It took her eyes a few moments to adjust to the sunlight and immediately, she noticed another black shape close to her on her right. Something bigger than Movenpick. It bounced before her, making a papery sound as it did.

It smelled of decay. The shape slowly bounced back, but did not go away. "Awk!" it said. Sankofa's eyes focused and she found herself looking at an enormous vulture, its wings casually spread. It stared back at her as if to say, "What are you going to do now?" To her right, now feet away, Movenpick yipped and paced back and forth, keeping his distance from both Sankofa and the vulture.

"I am The Adopted Daughter of Death," Sankofa told the vulture. "*You* are just a bird of death. Fly away. Or walk if you prefer. Just leave me." She got up and more dirt tumbled from her skin and her dress. Her satchel of things was gone. She brushed off the dirt from her arms, rubbed it from her face, spat it from her mouth. She coughed loudly, hacked mud from her throat and spat. She blew it from both her nostrils. She dug it from the sides of her eyes. When she looked up, the vulture was gone. For all its noise when it had moved away from her, it had taken to the air silent as an owl.

Sankofa stopped and stared at the area around her. She was in the bush, though she could hear vehicles on a road nearby. And she was standing in a shallow hole the length and width of her body. A shallow grave. Had they thought she was dead when they put her here? Or maybe they'd thought they were burying her alive. Or maybe the people of RoboTown weren't even the ones to bury her and some stranger had seen her lying in the road and put her here. But who would bury a child, especially one who was not dead? Life-Gen might. If only to see what would happen next. She glanced around cautiously.

Deciding she was as alone as she could get, she took a silent inventory of her entire body, flexing muscles and lifting her dirty dress off her legs to see if there were scratches or bruises . . . or stab wounds. She touched her ears and was glad to find she still wore her mother's earrings. She felt no pains or more than minor stings, but pain was a tricky beast, as she knew. Sometimes it took its time to officially arrive. But aside from a headache and a dull soreness in her fore-head, which was most likely where the drone's Taser had hit her, she was ok. She was alive.

She closed her eyes and tried bringing it forth. Would she still be able to? She could. Her world glowed green and the effortlessness of it was surprising. She tried shining even brighter. Then brighter. Then brighter. She lit up the road. And pulled it in. "I can do it so *easily* now," she whispered, looking at her hands. She glowed again, controlling the light so well that she could make it shine a foot from her and then pull it right back in. "What am I?" she said. But she didn't really care about that question. No. She was what she was and now after nearly dying, waking up in her own grave, and emerging from the soil, she was better.

She hugged herself and looked at Movenpick, wishing she could hug him, too. Movenpick yipped and trotted into the bush. Sankofa coughed again, hacked and spit out more mud and looked around her at the tall and robust forest. There were no plants around the spot where she'd lain. Barren, almost. No plants grew in the spot they'd chosen to bury her. Or maybe it had all died?

"I wonder . . ." she whispered, remembering. She simultaneously hoped in two directions as she reached into her right pocket. She wasn't surprised to find her wad of paper money. She held her breath as she reached into her left. "Dammit," she said when she touched the wood of the box. She spat out more dirty spit, tears rolling down her cheeks. "Dammit."

She heard a soft snort and turned around. Movenpick stood there, still waiting. "Thank you," she said. Movenpick fidgeted his paws and licked his chops. "Yes. Let's go."

Sankofa ran for the cover of dense trees, Movenpick trotting behind her. She wanted to get away from "her resting place." For an hour, she walked through forest. Still, as she walked, she kept an eye on the sky that she glimpsed between the leaves and branches, watching for Steel Brother's drones.

When she found the beautiful stream beside the large tree with several low growing branches thick enough to easily carry her weight, she knew she'd found a place to rest her tired lonely head. Even better, the area was bright with sunlight due to a large tree felled by a lightning strike. It was such a huge tree that its descent had taken down three other trees with it.

"I like this place," she said. Movenpick was already in the tree when she sat on the lower branch. She smiled for a moment, then she dropped the smile from her face and got up. She looked around until she spotted a smooth grey stone lodged beside the rotting mass of a fallen tree. She placed the seed on the hardest part of the tree's bark and then looked down her nose at it. Oval like a palm tree seed and etched as if its surface were trying to evolve into a circuit board. Always so so intriguing. She brought the stone down on it with all her strength. Then again. And again.

"Die!" she screamed each time she smashed at it. She laughed wildly and she cried, too. "DIE!"

Finally, she stopped. She looked down. The seed was in pieces like a giant cracked kernel of maize. She blinked. No, it wasn't. It was still whole, not even a dent. Not even her imagination could destroy it. She stood there staring at it for a long long time. She put it back in the box. Her hands felt heavy as she did so. The pull. As if it was telling her by sensation that it would never leave her again. Never. She returned to the giant tree she'd found, her face itchy with dried and fresh tears.

She sang a song with no words to herself as she dug a hole. She used a stick and then her hands and she dug it a foot deep. The she dropped the box into the hole. She buried it and patted the dirt down smooth. She stood back, looking down at the spot, half expecting a root to push it right back up. To even place it right back in her pocket. Nothing happened.

Sankofa stayed in this place for seven months. There were a few interesting things about this small patch of undisturbed forest. It was not near any villages or towns, so she didn't have to worry much about encountering any human beings. There was a road about a quarter of a mile away, but it was the type of road dominated by self-driving trucks and drivers who drove as if they expected spirits or witches to leap from the trees. There were three farms nearby, each run by old men who'd been working the land for decades. These old men had a farmer's code, for they had grown their vast farms on their own, and that code was one of secrecy.

One early evening, Sankofa had been out exploring further than usual and she'd smelled smoke. She followed the scent and this was how she found the three old men sitting around a fire smoking pipes and sharing stories. It was dark and she stayed in the shadows listening for a bit. They were talking about one of the old men's oldest granddaughters who'd come home pregnant and with a master's degree in engineering and how they didn't know whether to rejoice or die. They'd just decided to rejoice when Sankofa had boldly stepped into the firelight.

"Hello," she said. When none of the men had screamed or run off, she added, "May I join you?" It was the first time she'd spoken to another human being in months, and her voice came through loud and clear. They knew exactly who she was and they knew of what had gone down in RoboTown. "But we're on the farm, so secret stay here," was all one of the old men had said. And then one of the others made room for her and she sat down.

That night, Sankofa didn't join in in their discussion about the granddaughter who also didn't have a husband and didn't want one. She was happy to just listen. However, the next time she came across the old men in this same spot where the ashes of many fires remained, she talked to them about the way the land was exhaling. The farmers told her that it was great for their crops and that it would certainly be a good year. And one of the men brought her a sack of rice, a cooking pot, salt, some boiled eggs, and a jar of palm oil. They did not know that Sankofa could take care of herself, remembering how to live in the bush from her early days of being on her own. But the supplies were good and she was entitled to them being who she was, she knew it and she was glad the old men did, too.

"We respect the spirits," one of them said as she took the sack of goods. The next time she saw the men two weeks later, they had each brought her seeds and a plastic watering can. They called them "the basics," tomatoes, onions and cucumbers. And the next time, they gave her three yam cuttings.

Around the fallen trees, she cultivated a garden and the yam vines snaked over the lightning tree as if to embrace it. She ate well, slept well, laughed at Movenpick's habit of playing wildly in the grasses with dried palm fronds, and she enjoyed her time with the old farmers who seemed to genuinely enjoy her presence, too. In these days, she watched the things she planted grow and let the worst of her misadventures go. She mourned and then honored Alhaja by carving her name in the fallen lightning tree and speaking words of love to the birds, lizards, grasshoppers and spiders who were certainly listening.

She thought about her parents and brother as she always did and wondered what they'd think of all that had happened. She carved their names into the lightning tree, too. Not once during her time in the forest did she use her glow for more than killing off mosquitoes attacking her skin at night. The farmers were probably curious, but she never showed them her glow, except on that first night when they'd asked to see with their own old old wise eyes. Only on that day had they seemed to fear her.

Nevertheless, two hundred fifteen days after stepping out of her own shallow grave and making one for the seed in the box, she looked into the eyes of death . . . again. She was just coming from one of the evenings of chatting with the old men. She'd told them about how her garden was going and they'd all been impressed, saying that for someone who was fitted with the talent of taking life, she was also good at cultivating it. They'd all laughed. And she was still softly laughing to herself as she walked back to her home in the forest, Movenpick close behind. Movenpick went with her everywhere, even to visit the old men, but he never showed himself to them, so they only knew of him in legend.

She had a slight bellyache and she was wondering if she should eat a few mint leaves and call it an early night when Movenpick stopped and whined. He ran up a tree not far from their home. Then Sankofa noticed it, too. Every single creature in the forest had gone silent. It was dark so she saw nothing around her. Her night eyes and ears were sharp, so she usually felt safe in this forest. Until now. She froze, suddenly anxious, looking around, listening. She saw nothing. She moved faster, unsure of what she'd do when whatever, whomever it was revealed itself. What difference did it make if it was at her home or right here?

She made it to her garden and paused at her growing yam farm. She felt something creeping down her inner thigh. When she looked, she saw what might have been a line stretching toward her ankle. She squinted. She couldn't quite see it in the dark . . . but she could smell it. Blood. She gasped. If she'd scratched herself badly enough for blood to run down her leg, she certainly didn't feel it.

She was stepping up to the tree she and Movenpick

had been sleeping in for months and she was about to remove her wrapper when the leopard dropped in front of her. Its arrival was heavy yet perfect. A soft *thoom* and then *swipe* just missing Sankofa's chest. She fell back, somersaulted and was on her feet in less than a second. She ran. She knew this part of the forest so well that moving through it in the darkness was her advantage as the leopard came after her silent as a spirit. She slipped under a low branch, leapt over another. Leapt over the brook. Faster, faster, faster, she could hear it pursuing her like water flooding a creek. Focused and relentless.

Her mouth hung open as she fought to catch her breath; her mind was both clouded and sharp with adrenaline. She stumbled into the nearby road, the hardness of the concrete so unfamiliar after all these months that it hurt her feet. And that was when she finally remembered. What in Allah's name had she been running for? She turned to the forest and pushed for it to come. And for over a minute, it didn't.

The leopard burst into the road without making a sound. It came from directly in front of her. And because it happened to be a full moon and a clear night, she saw the great beast part the bushes and stride into view. Its head was low, its ears turned back and pressed close to its large spotted head. Its loose skin rolled and rippled over its muscular flesh.

Right there in the middle of the street, for the second time in her life, she faced death. However, she'd changed and grown since she left Wulugu; she had power now. It was just a matter of remembering, *truly* remembering and accepting. She stumbled back and her feet tangled. Down she went, sitting hard in the middle of the road. And still, she faced the leopard creeping so swiftly, so smoothly toward her. It had been months since she'd awoken in a shallow grave with complete control of her light. Months since she'd used her light for anything big.

However, time doesn't change the essence of what you are and Sankofa's essence had been forged and fused back home at the foot of that tree when the seed had fallen from the sky and she'd picked it up. She exhaled, letting it all go and letting it all in . . . what was in her killed her family, Alhaja, all those people who'd begged to be released from the shackle of life, insects, bats, drones, it protected her, it terrified others, it was from somewhere else, this seed . . . "All of it," she said, her face wet with tears. It hurt because so much of it was terrible and still it was hers. Regardless. "All of it."

It came easily and it came true.

As she lit up the road and forest in a thirty-foot radius, the leopard stopped, just at the beginning of the road. She could hear its guttural groan, as it placed a paw on the road. . . . and did not fall dead. She couldn't believe it. The strength of her light should have incinerated the beast to ash, leaving only bone.

"Why won't you *die*?" Sankofa whispered. A movement to her right caught her eye. Movenpick was also standing on the road not even ten feet away, bathed in her light. "Stay there, Movenpick," she shrieked. "Stay!" She stood up, facing the leopard. The beast had placed a second paw on the road. Today, Sankofa would die. She shined her light as brightly as she could shine it. A bat dropped to the ground beside her, dead, and she could hear the *plick* of beetles falling dead on the road.

The leopard was staring at her, close enough for her to see into its large eyes. In the green of her glow, those eyes opened up like windows. Sankofa gazed into them as the leopard crept closer and for a moment her world fell away and everything was green like the full moon above and the full moon inside her. In the years since she'd left home, she had only grown a few inches. She would always be a small girl from a small town. All this she saw in the leopard's eyes. It comforted her; this creature would send her home.

"Ok," she whispered.

The leopard was five feet away. Creeping. Sankofa frowned. It was twitching and blinking its eyes, its nostrils flaring wide. Its deep growl became a loud groan. It shook its head as if its nose were itching or burning. It stood up on its four legs, swaying a bit and looked piercingly at Sankofa. Then the leopard collapsed and did not get up.

Silence. Stillness.

"Yip!" she heard from her right.

"Movenpick," she whispered, her voice cracking. For a moment, she stared at the dead leopard, then with effort, she looked down at Movenpick. Slowly, very very slowly, she reached a shaky hand down. As she did, Movenpick lifted his head up. "Oh," she said, sniffing as tears of relief, shock and fatigue tumbled from her eyes. After so many years, the fox allowed her to touch him. The fur on his head was rough. "Who are you, my friend?" she whispered, wiping away a tear. "What are we?"

She pulled her light in and the road went back to being merely moonlit. The moment her light winked out and she looked up the road, she was gazing at another light. It came closer and closer. By the time she realized it was a bus, yet again, it was too late, and there she stood. Thankfully, the bus driver saw the girl in the moonlit road and slammed the brakes.

And it was in this way that a bus filled with passengers came to witness the small girl wearing a dress of near rags standing in the road with a massive dead leopard. Several of the passengers knew precisely who this was, despite rumors that she'd finally been killed. The bus driver also knew and he quickly jumped out to see if she was ok, for if this girl touched his bus they would all be stranded. A few passengers muttered under their breath about the driver's lack of professionalism by wasting their time helping the girl. Three teenagers recorded the entire moment with their phones and tablets and posted the footage online within minutes. Most stayed quiet and just watched through the bus windows.

As the bus driver and three of the women talked to her asking what happened and why she was out here, all Sankofa could think about was the fact that she could no longer return to her quiet garden. People had seen her and now they would come looking for her. They would find the farmers and ask questions and maybe one of them would say something. Again, she'd reached a moment where she knew it was time to leave.

"Thank you," she said, taking the pink tunic and trousers from an Indian woman who insisted she have them. The woman also gave her a box of maxi pads.

"Do you know how to use them?" the woman asked.

Sankofa nodded. She didn't but she could certainly figure it out.

"And you understand what it is, right?" the woman asked.

Sankofa nodded. "It's my period. I'm fourteen. I'd started to wonder if . . . I'm glad it has come."

The woman nodded, smiling. "It's good." She cocked her head. "I've heard about you, Sankofa. I am here working on a drone delivery system for some of the local hospitals and stories about you circulate there. Good stories."

"Really?" Sankofa said.

"Oh yes. One man had an aunt with terminal cancer who you . . . eased. He said you truly were like an angel."

One young man who didn't want to talk directly to Sankofa gave the Indian woman a bag of peanuts to give to her. A woman who'd been on her mobile phone the entire time offered Sankofa a large bottle of water, some flip-flops and a satchel to carry it all in. A man with an American accent gave her his near empty jar of shea butter. He'd rubbed a bit on his dark chapped hands first and she couldn't help but smile. Some of the other passengers pooled together money to give her. When the bus quickly pulled away leaving her with Movenpick (who'd leaped into the bushes until the bus was gone) and the body of the leopard, she turned and walked quickly into the bush.

She dug up the box and without bothering to clean off the remaining dirt or checking on the seed inside, she threw it in the new satchel the woman had given her. She preened and used her watering can to water her small garden. She washed her body and her blood-stained clothes in the stream. She rubbed shea butter on her clean skin. She figured out how to use a maxi pad. She gathered all her things, deciding to leave her bloodstained clothes and watering can behind. By night, Sankofa had left yet another home behind.

CHAPTER 10

NEW YEAR

They tell a story about Sankofa in many of the villages, towns and cities.

They say there once was a living child who was born to dead parents. Because her dead parents could not care for her, they took her to Death's doorstep and left her there. Her parents knew where this was because they were dead. They pinned a note to the child's blanket that explained they had given birth to a live child and that only Death would know what to do with her. They said she was beautiful, dark brown–skinned and perfect in every way and that when she cried, spiders, crickets and grasshoppers would sing to soothe her. They wrote that they wished they'd had her when they were alive and that fate was cruel.

Then they left the strange remarkable child there on death's doorway. Death knew the moment they left her because the smell of all things in Death's

household changed. The colors of marigold and per-
iwinkle began to appear in corners. And of course
the crickets, grasshoppers and spiders started
singing.

Nonetheless, Death did not open the door.
Death left the baby there. For six days. When the
baby did not die, Death grew curious. When Death
opened the door and saw the child, even she had to
admit that the child was unique. Death took the
child in and raised her until the child was seven
years old.

Death named her Sankofa because by the time
the child was of age, Sankofa had the ability to
send people back to their past, back to The Essence. Sankofa is The Adopted Daughter of Death.
And now she goes from town to town snatching
lives, sending them to her adoptive mother. You
see her face and you will soon see no more. She
looks nine years old because she is petite, but she is
actually thirteen.

Sankofa had once sat in a circle of young children and listened as a woman told this exact
version of her own story. No one there had any idea
that she was The Adopted Daughter of Death and she
was glad. She'd once watched a naked mad man in a

market frantically tell the story to himself. *His* telling made her seventeen years old. Another time, two teenage thieves told her the story as they tried to convince her that they could protect her from the powerful "remote control" of Death's Adopted Daughter . . . if she agreed to be their girlfriend. In their version of the story, they tried to scare Sankofa by exaggerating Death's Adopted Daughter's methods of killing. They said Sankofa carried a rusty machete that magically cut deep with the slightest pressure. The real Sankofa only rolled her eyes and walked off.

Some people said Death's Adopted Daughter was riddled with leprosy. Others said she was pretty, "like an American." Some said she was ugly like a girl raised in the bush. Some marked her as a blood-thirsty bald-headed adze, mythical vampires of the oldest stories who resulted from life's ugliest moments. Others said she wasn't human at all, that her blood had been tainted with radioactive gas by aliens who'd come to Earth through a black hole one night; that this was why she shined green. What they all agreed on was that wherever she went, she brought death. The only part of the shifting story that Sankofa hated was when people added the idea that her parents left her. Her parents *never ever* would have left her. She'd had the best parents in the world. Now, in her fourteenth year on earth, if there was one rule she lived by it was the fact that Stories were soothsayers, truth-tellers and liars.

She knew where she was going now. As New Year approached, she moved faster and more directly. When she needed rest, she stopped in towns and villages along the way. She accepted gifts. And though asked many times, only twice did she ease people into soft deaths. And only once did she kill in defense, days before, on Christmas night—a gateman whose mind was poisoned by the wild rumors that preceded her. She met more farmers and they were almost always kind, and when they weren't, they at least knew to stay out of her way. She had no other trouble. And Movenpick had finally decided she was worthy of his full trust, coming close to sleep beside her at night, finally, and always following from a slight distance when they travelled during the day. No one gave Movenpick any trouble, either.

Sankofa arrived at the border on New Year's morning. She was wearing her long yellow skirt, matching top embroidered with expensive lace and a purple and yellow headband made of twisted cloth. She'd acquired another simpler green wrapper and top and had worn that all week, saving this one from Christmas for the day she entered Wulugu. She wanted to arrive in style.

The trees looked different. So did the road. It was so black that it looked like it led to another dimension. The stripes on it were so yellow that they looked like the paths of shooting stars. But this was the road that led into the town of Wulugu. At least what used to be Wulugu. Who knew what Sankofa would find here? Even at this hour, the road was busy with autonomous delivery and transport trucks and personal vehicles. She stood to the side of the road remembering. Not a mile away was the place where her normal life had ended.

"We're back," she said to Movenpick, who stood right beside her. She could see the top of the mosque in the distance up the road, so there was still something left. "Let's go home."

Her stomach was growling, but she was too excited to care. As she walked, old darkened memories tried to sneak into her mind, her mother's face, her father's voice, her brother's laugh. Her heart fluttered and she shut her eyes as she walked. The feeling passed and she was happy again. Movenpick trotted at her heels like a dog.

There were still ghosts in Wulugu and Sankofa was relieved. She felt them as she strolled into town, lingering in shadows, between buildings, on front steps. Reminders that everything that had happened truly happened, no matter how much had been covered up, rebuilt, replaced, reorganized. As she came up the road and approached the mosque, she passed several people leaving it. She recognized no one and she was glad when no one recognized her. And she was glad Movenpick stuck close.

She passed a small and very empty market area. This place looked the same, though it wasn't. The old table outside a closed restaurant where in the evening men would sit outside and play cards and smoke cigarettes was still there. She wondered if it still had the same purpose. The narrow dirt road that ran through town was now paved with fresh asphalt and used by people on foot and on bicycles instead of cars.

There was joy in the air. And beyond the homes and buildings on the right were the shea tree farms, Sankofa knew. A few years wouldn't matter much to trees; if anywhere looked the same, it would be the shea farms. She stopped at one of the random shea trees that grew in the town square. She stepped closer. Carved into its trunk was "#AfricansAreNot-LabRats". She ran her hand over it, wondering who'd taken the time to carve it. *Probably someone who's long moved on,* she thought.

She passed Wulugu's biggest hotel and, now twice the size as it had been, it was much nicer than she remembered. It even looked like it now had running water and more generators. And there was a very new-looking pharmacy attached, a big advertisement for LifeGen nasal spray in the window. Sankofa stopped at this, frowning. She glanced up, surveying the sky.

Two dark-skinned tall women dressed in stylish western jeans, T-shirts and gym shoes and with long perfectly coiffed dreadlocks came out of the hotel entrance, giggling as they looked at their mobile phones. When they noticed Sankofa they grinned. "Good morning," they said to Sankofa, walking in the direction she'd come from. They had American accents. Why were Americans here?

"Good morning," Sankofa said, smiling back.

"Cute dog," one of them said. She held up her phone, took a photo of Movenpick and then they both were on their way. Sankofa watched them go for a moment and then she moved on.

When she reached her home and knocked on the door, no one answered. Instead, the door swung open and the smell of dust and abandonment wafted out. She stood there looking inside, Movenpick beside her. If she'd needed even one hint of what had transpired in Wulugu six years ago, here it was. Every single home she'd passed up to this point, every single building, every booth in the women's market, the bicycle shop, everything was occupied. Different faces, different families, but people. Except this house.

Sankofa looked at Movenpick. "They've tried so hard to move on," she muttered. Across the street, she eyed a woman sitting on her porch watching her. She waved and smiled and the woman slowly waved back. Sankofa had no idea who that woman was. The house itself hadn't even been there when she left. She went inside.

The house had been gutted. Every piece of furniture, every rug, her brother's collection of wooden carvings, old photos, everything. It was just an unoccupied home now. Left to crumble back to the dust it came from on its own. However, for Sankofa, it was full. Right there was where her mother used to sit and listen to audiobooks on her mobile phone when she could get it to work. Right there was where her brother would lay out the pages of his school assignments and work his way meticulously through them until dinnertime. Right there was the spot in the kitchen where his father would make a pile of the best shea fruits that fell from the tree in the backyard, the tree that was not a farm tree, but the family tree.

And in the back of the house was the family tree that Sankofa used to secretly climb and hide in for hours. It was taller now, and wider, its branches healthily green with long leathery leaves and unripe plum-sized shea fruit. At its base was where the seed had fallen on her "sky words" and later the box had been pushed through the soil.

She gasped, realizing. "My 'sky words,'" she whispered, brushing a sandaled foot over the dirt where she used to draw them. She hadn't thought about them in over a decade. She blinked. "Did my drawings bring the . . ." She frowned and decided it didn't matter. Not right now.

Sankofa slowly walked up to the spot before the tree. She knelt down. Movenpick trotted past her and easily climbed up the rough trunk and sat on a thick branch. With her small hands, she started digging.

There was only one place on Earth where this thing would be at rest, where this thing would allow *her* to rest. The red soil was soft, yielding and moist as her fingers dug into it. She inhaled its fragrant aroma, feeling herself begin to glow. Above, the tree seemed to lean over her. Her fingers dug deeper into the soil and soon, she felt something beneath it. Solid, but moving. She did not pull her hands away. Instead, she let it firmly grasp her hand.

The tree's root, a brownish reddish thing, snaked up. With her free hand, Sankofa reached into the pocket of her worn pink pants and brought out the box. The root wavered before her and then stopped, waiting.

"What are you," she asked it. "The devil? A demon?" *An alien?* She blinked, knowing this was true. Knowing that her "sky words" were at least part of why it had come here, to this specific spot. How she'd been able to see and duplicate what she saw in the stars was a question she'd ask herself for a long time. "Fatima," she said. "My name is Fatima Okwan." *But I'm Sankofa, too,* she thought. *Always.* "Fatima," she said again, and the faces of her father, mother and brother shined brightly in her mind for just a moment before fading back to the washed-out images they had been since she'd left.

She cast the box into the hole and spat on it. "Stay

there. I don't want you. You weren't a gift, you were a curse." Her shoulders slumped as she felt something leave her. The waiting roots slid almost lovingly around the box, their roughness grating softly against the box's wood, a sound Sankofa would remember for the rest of her life. Then their grip tightened, crushing the box and seed. She saw the seed inside crack in two just before it all descended quickly into the dirt, pulled down by some force Sankofa would never fully understand.

Sankofa felt her legs weaken and she sat down in front of the hole and stared at it. She looked past the hole, at the tree. She looked past the tree and only saw the farm. For a moment, she recalled her father walking in from the farm, a sack of personally picked shea nuts over his shoulder. He always used these ones to make the shea butter his family spread on their skin. Her heart ached.

She put down her satchel and stretched out on the ground, flat, her face to the soil. For an hour, she sat facing the tree, remembering and remembering. No mental walls. No turning away. Her body softly glowing.

She stayed home, curling up on the bare floor and falling into a deep well-earned slumber. Hours later, her empty stomach woke her. It was dark, so she brought forth her glow to light the room. She stretched and went outside to the backyard. Movenpick was in the tree looking down at her. She climbed up to join him. When she looked out over the shea tree farm she was met with an eerie sight. She gasped, clutching the tree's trunk so she didn't fall.

In the night, the view was like a galaxy of green stars. They shined from the base of almost all the trees. All except the base of hers, because *her* seed had been crushed. No one had spent time in the trees as she did. Had that been why the seed was offered to her? Or was it solely because of her "sky words"? What would *these* grow into? And now that LifeGen had entrenched itself in Wulugu, were they going to harvest them? International corporate-level remote control.

"That would be bad," she muttered.

And so she brought forth her light. When she did, all the seeds glowing in the soil brightened. She pushed her light to grow brighter. The seeds brightened some more. Then some more.

Then even brighter. And this time, she did it on purpose.